LETICIA - THE GRIEVING BRIDE

FROM BRAVE NURSES TO COURAGEOUS BRIDES

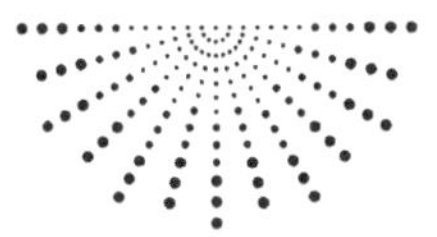

INDIANA WAKE

SWEETBOOKHUB.COM

FROM BRAVE NURSES TO COURAGEOUS BRIDES

Welcome to this new series of three books for you my wonderful readers.

Each of these books is a complete story, with the journey of the three of them running through the whole series. The three friends were nurses who worked on the battlefields from 1861 to 1865. After the war, they found themselves lost and with little future.

They take a chance to head west to find love and a new life but things don't all go as they had hoped.

Will they find happiness, love, and all they dreamed of, or have they found a worse life than the one they left?

Read on for Leticia's Story.

Books in the series:

Carolyn – The Orphaned Bride

Margaret – The Big Beautiful Bride

Leticia – The Grieving Bride

CHAPTER ONE

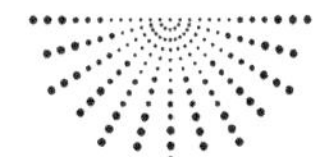

Leticia rubbed her palms together and blew into them for warmth. It had rained the night before, the air was chilly and the path was muddy. There was a soft squishing sound with every step she took. Looking down, she was regretting wearing her nice pair of white shoes to visit the town.

Leticia hated wearing shoes except when necessary, but Margaret had said that they looked good on her. It was silly, but she wanted to look good. However, due to the rain, they were stained with mud, even the pretty bow on the top.

Leticia exhaled and looked up at the sky. It was bright out that morning, but the sun was hiding behind clouds and not that warm.

"The perfect weather for a stroll around town," she said with a sigh. "If only my shoes weren't ruined."

Carolyn and Margaret were starting to notice the change in her demeanor. Gently teasing her because she was dressing differently, her hair was neat all of the time, and she wore shoes more than she usually did, especially to town. They guessed that she had grown bored since they were always with their beaus. Leticia let them believe that, but she knew they were completely wrong.

To get to town, she had to pass the local doctors who ran a clinic from his house. A week ago, she had run into Oliver, the doctor was standing in front of his house. It had been completely coincidental, but she noticed that her heart skipped a beat when she laid eyes on him. Her normal response to things she could not explain was to ignore them, but this time, she decided not to. So, to confirm just how much effect Oliver had on her, Leticia tried to run into him again. It took three days, but she successfully bumped into him on the road. To her surprise, not only did her heart skip a beat, but she was sure that she felt butterflies in her stomach when he smiled at her.

It all started at the dance. At least, that was as far back as Leticia could trace the change in her feelings.

Two weeks ago, she had apologized to Oliver for slapping him across the face and misjudging him. Oliver had accepted her apology and had even asked her to a dance. During the night, they danced twice, and their conversations were light and filled with laughter. Oliver was always quick to offer his help, and somehow, Leticia had managed to look past the fact that the local doctor reminded her so much of the man she once loved. The conversations she had with Oliver had convinced her that he and Dwight were two completely different people. Apart from the fact that they had the same exact eyes, they were nothing alike.

Oliver seemed warmer. Obviously kind. Leticia liked those traits about him. It was the first time in a long time that she had been curious about somebody. In the last two weeks, she had met Oliver five times and she recalled everything about their encounters. A chuckle escaped her as she remembered how her cheeks hurt because she couldn't stop smiling, how she replayed their conversations at every chance she got, how Carolyn and Margaret were starting to suspect her, and how she was always looking forward to seeing him again.

Leticia had convinced herself that Oliver liked her too. Not just as a friend that he was helping with her trauma, but as a woman. That's what she wanted to believe. It made the scenarios in her head romantic. Leticia had told him about her dreams and Oliver had recommended some soothing herbs for her to take before bed. He made sure to ask her about it every time they met.

Was she reading too much into it? How she hoped not, for she felt her heart could be broken once more if the doctor rejected her.

"Leticia, it's so nice to see you today."

There was only one person with that voice and hearing it sent tingles down her spine. Leticia smiled and tucked the loose strands of her blonde hair behind her ear as she turned around slowly. It had been three days since she had last seen Oliver and she sighed in relief, thankful that she had decided to take her walk today.

"Good morning, Doctor Randall," Leticia beamed. "A beautiful morning, isn't it?" She lowered her eyes for the handsome and broad-shouldered man always took her breath away. Despite the grey in his hair, he had a face that drew her glance and icy blue eyes that still reminded her of Dwight.

"It is indeed," he answered, placing his arms behind his back. "I see you're on your way to town."

Leticia glanced at the basket in her hand. "I am. It's for Edwin."

Oliver gestured for them to keep walking. He stayed by her side, keeping his arms behind him as they strolled down the path. "Edwin?" he asked. "Is he all right?"

"Oh, he's fine. I am buying foodstuffs for a dinner we're hosting in a couple of days. Edwin wishes to marry Margaret. We're celebrating it, so Carolyn and I are setting everything up and getting things ready."

"A party? That's wonderful. I'm sure Margaret's thrilled by the news."

"She doesn't know," Leticia answered. "Edwin came to Carolyn and me in secret."

"Ah," Oliver said softly. "I'd love to see her reaction to his proposal."

"You can," Leticia said without sparing a minute to think about it. "I'd like to invite you to the dinner. Please. I'd be glad if you came."

Oliver smiled. "Absolutely. I'll be there."

It felt like Leticia had achieved a great feat. Inviting Oliver to dinner was a big step for her, and seeing how desperate she had been for him to say yes, it confirmed how much she had grown to like him. It made sense that she thought about him all of the time.

Leticia slowed her pace and walked two steps behind Oliver. She watched him, secretly admiring his features. Thankfully, his eyes didn't affect her as much as they used to. The silver-tone in his brown hair seemed to have increased. Oliver liked to keep his hair out of his face. He maintained his ducktail haircut, and his face was neatly shaved.

She had asked around about Oliver from some of the townsfolk, and they had nothing but good things to say about him. Oliver was in his early forties, he loved the church, loved his daughter, and was charitable. The mere thought that he might like her excited Leticia. If only there was a way to confirm it.

"Is it weird that I cannot seem to get our dance off my mind?" Oliver asked.

"What?" Leticia blurted out and turned to him. *What did that mean?*

CHAPTER TWO

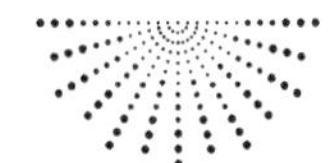

*D*id that mean that he liked her? Was this the proof she had sought? Her face must have shown confusion for it crossed his features.

"Our dance," Oliver repeated. "I enjoyed it, very much. That was the first time in a long time that I danced with someone and it was very nice. It might seem weird, but I hope we get to do it again soon."

Leticia's cheek burned. She placed her palm on her left cheek and stared at the ground. Was that the confirmation she needed? Did Oliver just admit that he liked her?

Leticia shook her head vigorously and cleared her throat. It was risky to get ahead of herself.

"I'm happy for Edwin and Margaret, by the way," Oliver said, changing the subject. "They seem so happy together, and I'm proud of that. Just a month ago, Edwin was willing to give up on life, but Margaret managed to convince him to give life another go. It takes love to do that."

"Well, Margaret is just love and optimism wrapped in the body of a woman with beautiful red hair. She sees the good in everything and every situation, and regardless of what she has been through, she's still pushing through with a smile on her face. She and Carolyn are the best things in my life and I learn a lot from them. I'm glad Margaret and Edwin are happy.

Oliver glanced at her. "I'm glad too. I also hope that she and Edwin can make their union work. It's going to be tough – I mean, it is already tough, but they can pull through regardless of Edwin's blindness."

"I believe so too," Leticia said. "I do. It needs to work, honestly, because I look up to them for... hope." *Why had she said that?*

Leticia glanced at Oliver but ground to a halt when she noticed that he had stopped walking. She slowed down and stood in front of him, concerned.

"Is there a problem, Oliver?" she asked, wondering why he was staring at her so intently.

"I would like to officially ask to court you, Leticia," Oliver announced.

Leticia's heart not only skipped a beat, but its palpitations were so loud, that she didn't she'd think she heard him correctly. She tilted her head to the side and took a step forward.

"I'm sorry, Doctor Randall. I wasn't listening... I don't think I heard you properly. What did you say?"

"I'd like to court you, Leticia." There was a big smile on his face. "I want to get to know you better."

It was the confirmation she needed. It had to be. Why else would Oliver ask to court her if he didn't like her as she liked him? But contrary to what Leticia expected, she wasn't excited by the news. She felt scared and confused. Where was her heart really at?

There was no doubt that she liked Oliver, but deep down, Leticia was still in love with Dwight. He was the only thing she held dearly to her heart. She had let the new feelings for the doctor distract her from that fact, which helped tremendously because she had stopped having nightmares. But it didn't change the fact that she loved Dwight.

"Leticia?"

"I'd love to," Leticia said, surprising herself.

It seemed her heart and her head were not on the same page. It was Oliver. Carolyn and Margaret liked him, he was handsome and kind. Leticia had always wished for even a quarter of Margaret's optimism and it didn't seem right to turn away a good man. Dwight wasn't coming back either. Was there any need to stop herself from pursuing something new?

Oliver sighed in relief and smiled. "Are you sure? You looked bothered by my request. I wouldn't want to force you into something you don't want to do."

Leticia shook her head. "I want to, Doctor Randall. Life away from old troubles has renewed my belief and hope for the future. You have my permission."

"Thank you," Oliver said with a slight bow. "I have to meet a patient here," he said, pointing at the house to his right. "I'll see you at the dinner?"

"I'll be expecting you," Leticia said. "Have a nice day, Doctor Randall."

"Please. I think we're past the formalities now," Oliver said. "Call me Oliver, Leticia."

Leticia nodded. "Have a nice day, Oliver."

"You too, Leticia."

Oliver waved at her as he walked up the short stairs. Leticia stood there and watched him converse with someone before he was ushered into the house. She made her way down the path, her chest a tad lighter and far warmer. Perhaps she too could get her own happy ending. Perhaps, she had found her beau, just like Carolyn and Margaret had.

"Perhaps..." she whispered with a wide grin on her face and yet, there was a deep fear that reared its ugly head and told her something would go wrong.

CHAPTER THREE

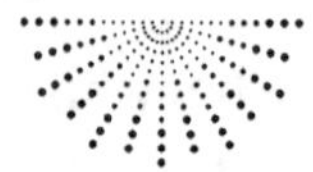

Margaret stood in the corner of the living room, watching Edwin. She rapped her fingers on the wall softly, knowing it would let him know she was there as she made sure she was close enough to him in case he needed her, but not too close to bother him.

Despite his new blindness, Edwin had insisted on feeding himself, and no amount of arguing convinced him otherwise. He had improved so much since he allowed them to know of his condition. Physically, too, he was stronger. Capable of walking around with a cane. It took a while, but he had mapped out the house. Though he still needed her help with a lot of things, and

Margaret was glad that she could help, he was getting more comfortable with his situation.

"I know you're there, Maggie," Edwin said and turned around, his gaze darting. "I can hear you."

Margaret held her breath. "Hear what?"

Edwin turned back around, pushing the small table away from him. "I don't know. I can just kind of sense you. I thought you said you wanted to do some laundry?"

"I was planning to," Margaret said.

Edwin picked up his cane and rose to his feet. "Let me guess. You were waiting around to see if I needed something, weren't you?"

Margaret scurried to his side and held his arm. "Where are you going?"

"To the bed, Maggie." Edwin smiled. "I can do it myself."

"I know you can."

"Then how about you let go of my arm, young lady?" Edwin asked.

"Why? I'd like to help."

"That's sweet. But you're treating me like a child, Margaret Sampson. Although I like it when we hold hands, I can walk to the bed myself, my love. Having said that, how about you let go of my arm" – Edwin gently pried his arm away from her grasp – "And let me show you?"

Margaret hesitated before letting go of his arm. "All right then, Edwin. Be careful."

"I'll try."

A knock on the door stopped them both in their tracks.

"I'll get it," Margaret said.

Edwin nodded and proceeded into the room while Margaret strolled to the door. She opened it slightly to take a peek and then pulled the door open when she recognized the face.

"Hello, Maggie," Samantha beamed. "You look lovely this morning. I love that dress on you."

"Good morning, Sam," Margaret answered with a smile. "Thank you. I think you look lovely as well. Please come in. Edwin just went into the room. I'll let him know you're here."

"Thank you," Samantha said.

"Is that Sam?"

Margaret turned around to see Edwin standing in the middle of the living room.

"Oh, yes," she answered.

Samantha strolled into the room and stopped in front of him. She had a habit of examining his face for a few seconds before she said anything. Margaret had noticed it on two other occasions when Sam came around to check up on him. She figured Sam did it out of habit. As a doctor like her father, it was her job to diagnose people.

"Hello, Edwin," Samantha said. "How are you?"

"Very well," Edwin said. "How are you?"

"I'm good."

Edwin stretched his hand to the side and wiggled his fingers gently. It was his signal to Margaret, asking her to take his hand. Margaret took the hint and stood by his side.

"My checkup isn't until tomorrow," Edwin continued. "Should I be worried about something?"

Samantha shrugged her shoulders. She crossed to a chair and sat. "No. I just came to see you."

Margaret led Edwin across the room and helped him sit on the chair on the other side. She smiled, amused by Sam's carefree demeanor. Margaret recalled that period two months ago when she had been jealous and furious at Samantha because she thought Samantha and Edwin were lovers. Now, it all seemed so absurd. Samantha might not be willing to admit it, but Edwin was technically her closest friend in the community. She always found an excuse to visit them.

Like a week ago when Sam had visited Margaret at the restaurant. She had come to eat, but she didn't leave until the restaurant closed. She helped them clean the tables, and arrange the chairs before she left. Margaret liked the fact that Sam considered them friends. All she liked to do was work at her father's clinic. But lately, she had been all right with stopping by from time to time.

Edwin shifted to the end of his chair. "You only came to visit? Why don't I believe you?"

Samantha scoffed. "I came to see how you were doing. Can I not do that?"

"Oh, you can. But it's morning, and given how busy you and Doctor Randall are these days, you must have patients to see. That would mean you don't have time to spare."

Samantha gave Margaret a knowing look and then smiled. "All right, fine. I have some information that I think would be of great benefit to you, Edwin."

"Ah, of course," Edwin said. "I'm listening, Sam."

Maggie watched him closely, there was worry in the lines around his face but this would be good news... wouldn't it?

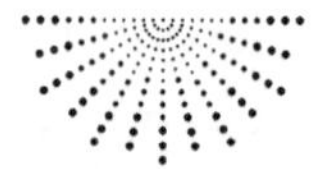

argaret adjusted in her seat and straightened her back, holding her breath in anticipation, while Sam locked her fingers together and placed her arms on her knees.

"I did some research over the last week, and I have a suggestion for you, Edwin." Samantha cleared her throat. "Even though the options are limited, there are some things you could be doing right now to help your situation. For a start, you could learn Braille."

Margaret tilted her head sideways. "Braille?"

Samantha nodded. "Yes Braille. It is a way for you to learn how to read again, Edwin."

Edwin shook his head and Margaret could see his frustration.

"That makes no sense, I can't see." Edwin's jaw was clenched tightly.

"No, but you can feel. Louis Braille developed a system of raised dots to form letters and therefore, words. Trust me, you can do this and it will present a lot of opportunities."

Margaret watched Edwin, while he listened in silence. Lately, he didn't like to talk about things that he could or could not do.

"Edwin," Sam continued. "I know you might still not be ready to try something new, but I thought I should come and inform you about it before I ask my father for help. It might seem difficult, but you can do it."

Edwin slowly leaned into the chair and sighed. "I'm ready for anything, Sam. Honestly, I will admit that trying something new scares me, but I want to try it. I don't want to give up like I am so used to doing. So, I'll do it. I have Maggie by my side. That's enough for me."

Margaret squeezed his arm. "I'm not going anywhere, Edwin. We'll figure this out together. Whatever it is you want to do, we'll do it together. We have passed through

– what I think are the dark days of our lives. Those days are far behind us. I want to believe that this is the start of a new future here in a new town. Whatever you decide to do, I'm sure you will do well, and I will be here to cheer you on."

Edwin moved closer to Margaret and placed his head on her shoulder. "That's all I need to hear, Maggie. I'll work hard, so you don't have to worry about me. I also need to start thinking about the future and I think this is a good start. It only matters this much to me as long as I have you close to me."

"Ah, so you admit you're doing this for Maggie?" Samantha teased.

"Yes, I am," Edwin answered and lifted his head. "If she left me alone, I would probably still be in that cottage, wasting my life away and slowly killing myself. She's the reason I'm still here, and as such, I'm living for her, and I'll achieve anything for her."

Margaret blushed. She leaned in and placed a peck on Edwin's cheek. "We have each other. That's all that matters."

"Well, I should be on my way," Samantha said, rising to her feet. "I'll confer with my father, and I will be back when I have more details. Please take care of yourselves and if you need anything, you know where to find me."

Margaret rose to her feet. "Thank you so much, Sam. We really appreciate all that you do for us and we don't take it for granted."

"No need to thank me, Maggie. That's what friends do for each other, and I'm happy to think of the three of us as friends. I'll be in touch."

"Thank you, Sam," Edwin said.

Margaret walked Samantha to the door and then returned to Edwin's side. They sat quietly in each other's arms for a while before Edwin rose to his feet. Margaret made to stand up too, but Edwin lifted his finger in the air.

"Maggie, sit," he said. "I just need to ease myself. I'll be back shortly."

"Oh, I actually need to do some laundry," Margaret answered. "Let's just walk to the backyard together."

"No," Edwin said. "Don't you need to get to the restaurant? You're going to be late for work you know."

"I won't," she answered. "Don't worry about it."

"Well, you haven't had your breakfast yet," Edwin said, bringing his arm to his hip. "You hovered so much this morning because I didn't let you feed me, and when I asked you to eat with me, you said you had to do laundry. I know you weren't telling the truth because you stood at the corner, watching me eat. Maggie..."

Margaret recognized the warning tone. "Fine, fine. I'll stay back and have breakfast while you go do what you want to do."

"Don't follow me," Edwin asked.

"I won't."

"You promise?"

"What if you trip and fall on your face?"

"If I do, I'll stand up again."

"What if..."

"Maggie."

"Fine." Margaret threw her hands in the air and sat back down. "I just want to spend time with you, but it's fine. If you need anything, just call for me."

"I will." Edwin smiled. "I love you."

Margaret crossed her arms and watched silently as Edwin stood there, waiting for her response. He wasn't going to budge until she said something, but she remained quiet. She was amused by the situation.

"Maggie, don't make me sit on you."

Margaret giggled. "Love you, too. Now go."

"Good. Now, eat."

Margaret watched him find his way around the house with a proud smile on her face. She was happy that Edwin had no problem negotiating his way around the house. They had practiced together, but still, she wanted to be everywhere with him.

Margaret wasn't burdened by Edwin's dependence on her for basic things. She loved it. She loved him. However, she knew it frustrated him, that he worried about supporting her. Now, they were heading into a new adventure her biggest fear was that he would give up, that he would feel unable to support her and lose faith. How she prayed that this new Braille would help him feel enough.

CHAPTER FIVE

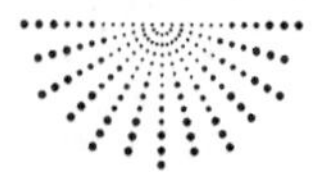

The most common compliment Leticia received in the twenty-two years that she had lived was that people loved how confident she looked and sounded. But sitting in Oliver's wagon, as he drove down the road, she was anything but, her palms were sweaty, and she couldn't find any words to say.

Oliver had picked her up at the restaurant late in the afternoon. Leticia had practically snuck out, dressed nicely, with her blonde hair tied in a high ponytail. She had avoided Carolyn and Margaret's questions and left with no explanation. They surely knew something was up, but she couldn't tell them... yet. She hadn't had the time, and she figured it was too soon to be gushing about Oliver, it still felt like a betrayal of Dwight. She needed to be sure that this was real and that it was reciprocated before she took that step.

"Leticia, are you all right?" Oliver asked her.

Leticia took a breath. "What do you mean?"

Oliver glanced at her. "You don't seem like yourself. You seem tense. Are you cold?"

"No, no, I'm not. I'm rather hot, on the contrary," she replied. "I just don't like the silence. We've been sitting in the wagon for a while, and all I hear are the sounds of the horses trotting and the wheels turning. I'm nervous, I admit. But we're too quiet, is all."

"Oh, what do you want to talk about then?" Oliver asked, keeping his eyes on the road.

Leticia bit her lower lip. "I don't know. I can't think of anything and I feel bad because I mentioned it."

Oliver chuckled and shook his head. "The dreams you keep having. Let's talk about that."

"The dreams?"

"The repetitive ones," Oliver answered. "The ones we've been talking about all this time? You know you haven't quite told me what they are about. I might be able to help you better if I knew."

"Oh, those dreams…"

What Oliver didn't know was that he had already been a big help. Leticia wasn't having the dreams anymore because she was so distracted by him.

"Leticia?" Oliver called her softly. "Why do you look so distracted?"

Leticia shook her head. "I'm sorry. I don't have the dreams anymore. I was surprised that I hadn't thought about them for a while."

"Well, do you want to tell me what they were about?"

She certainly didn't. Bringing up Dwight right now would not help. "Well, it's really not that important," she stuttered. "It's just a good dream that becomes terrifying just before I wake up. The good news is I don't have it anymore."

"That's good. I was glad to be of help."

If Leticia didn't like Oliver that much, she might have considered telling him what the dream was about. But it didn't feel right. Their relationship was still fresh. Talking about dead first loves didn't seem all that…

romantic, especially for their first evening together since they began courting. Besides, Oliver knew a great deal about her, but she knew next to nothing about his private life. She wanted to hear about him.

The wagon slowed them when they approached a meadow sloping down to a stream with several white elm trees dotted along the bank. Leticia took in a breath and smiled at the scenery. It was shady, the perfect spot she could fall asleep in. Leticia loved sitting under the shade of a big tree. It always felt like a warm hug from nature. There was no way Oliver knew that.

"Why did you choose this place?" she asked him.

"Well, I like it. I was hoping you liked it too. The elm's leaves seem to sparkle across the back of the creek in the wake of the falling sun. I think it's a pretty sight."

"It's a beautiful sight," Leticia said. "There is one downside to this though."

Oliver's forehead furrowed. "What is it?"

"I might fall asleep," Leticia said and chuckled. "But on the other hand, I have never noticed this place on my travels around Appleton. I love it. And yes, the leaves seem to sparkle. It's peaceful. You'd expect a place like this to have many people. Do you know what this place is perfect for?"

"A picnic?"

"Exactly." Leticia chuckled again. "A nice picnic."

Oliver stepped down, came around, and offered her his hand. A spark of heat traveled up her arm as he helped her down and his hand stayed on hers a little longer than needed as she looked into his eyes. It was safe to say that she was a little nervous as she stepped off the wagon and walked side-by-side holding hands and yet, it was also exciting.

He led her to the edge of the creek and lay a blanket down. Leticia sat on it and made herself comfortable by leaning on the trunk of a tree. Oliver sat by her side and leaned on the tree too. This time, Leticia was comfortable with the silence. She loved the view of the creek, as it flowed and disappeared into the distant view. She wished they had planned a picnic instead. It would have been fun.

"Can I tell you something?" Oliver said, breaking the silence.

Leticia turned her head to him. "You can tell me anything."

"This moment," he started. "Us... here, listening to the silence and enjoying the view and the moment. This was a memory I wanted to create with my late wife. I wanted us to share such a moment. It was little things like this that make everything seem simple. What's so bad about having a moment like this? Sitting in silence and ignoring all the worries of the world?"

"Nothing at all," Leticia said. "Why didn't you? What stopped you from creating this memory with your late wife?"

"Oh, Freya hated Appleton." Oliver shrugged. "She hated the town so much. She claimed it smelt of horses, manure, and rotting food."

"What?" Leticia blurted. "Appleton is the best place I've been in. Ever. I'm not exaggerating when I say I have no plans of leaving this place. I am grateful that we found this town. What's there not to like? Fresh food, wonderful people, the weather's nice... it's heaven to me. Heaven on Earth, given where I'm coming from."

Oliver chuckled. "I like listening to you talk. You are bold, and you don't hesitate to say exactly what's on your mind. I learned that the hard way." He winked.

Leticia blushed. "What happened to Sam's mom?" she asked.

Oliver took in a deep breath. "Well, she wanted us to move. She wanted to leave the town. But I didn't, so we didn't quite get along well. Ultimately, she left me and left on her own. She was determined to leave, and I couldn't stop her. She's gone now, taken by the Lord too young. I heard it was an infection but do you know what hurts me most?"

"What?" Leticia asked curiously.

"She didn't even try to take Samantha. She didn't fight for her. When she had made up her mind, I told her, I said you can leave, but you're not taking my daughter. And she just left. Without a moment to reconsider, Freya just left. I was in a dark place for a long time after that. I didn't understand what changed so suddenly. I wanted to love Freya for the rest of my life, I had planned it all out. But she didn't even want to fight for it. She had a plan too, and it didn't involve Samantha or me."

Leticia stared directly at him and felt a pang in her heart. Oliver was being vulnerable with her. He had no issue talking about his past, and Leticia didn't see a reason to hold back anymore.

"Did you tell me about your wife because you want me to tell you about my dreams?" she asked, squinting her eyes to observe him closely.

Oliver met her gaze and chuckled. "I might have. A part of me thinks you have a similar story to tell. One that haunts you too, and I would like to hear it. What brought you and everyone else that came with you to Appleton? What's your dream about, Leticia?"

Leticia leaned back on the tree and sighed loudly. "My dream... I think it's more of a nightmare, or it's something in between. It's about my first love. His name was Dwight. My dream always starts off well. Dwight and I were the perfect match. We loved each other, and his parents loved me too. We had so many happy memories together."

"Is that what you dream about? The fond memories with Dwight?"

"At first. The dream is more like a recap of my life with him. It's rosy at the beginning and horrible at the end. Dwight died, Oliver. During the war. I saw his body. His burnt-up body when they brought him in. Sometimes I wish I had listened to Margaret when she asked me not to go out there, not to see him. But I was stubborn. I pried my hands from hers and I rushed to the tent. I could barely recognize him, half of his face was gone. That's the last thing I always see. His burned body. That's what I wake up to."

"That sounds horrible," Oliver commented. "I'm sorry."

"It's all right. I haven't had the dream in a while, so I'm getting over it. But that's the story. Our stories might not be identical, but I know what it's like to love and to lose the most important person in one's life. It takes its toll on you."

Oliver sat up. "There is something I want to know, Leticia. What brought you to Appleton... exactly?"

Leticia's heart skipped a beat. "Huh?"

"There are rumors, but no one knows why exactly you came here. You were a nurse during the war."

"I was," Leticia answered.

"Why settle down in a small town like Appleton then? There are many other places you could be, where you could put your skills to work. Plus, you said that being here is like heaven compared to where you're coming from. Where exactly are you coming from that makes a small town like this feel like heaven?"

Leticia looked away and drew in a raggedy breath. Why was he interested in her past all of a sudden? His questions were so specific, that Leticia couldn't help but wonder if he had heard something bad. The breath froze in her throat and her chest felt tight. If he found out he would hate her, he would want no more to do with her.

"You say it like there's a big story," Leticia managed to say.

Oliver reached for her hand and took it. "You can trust me, Leticia. I mean you no harm. I'm only trying to get to know you better. Be honest with me."

"It's nothing special, Oliver. Carolyn, Maggie, and I simply followed Sherman. He came on a mission to South Dakota. You know Sherman and Carolyn are in love. They are going to get married soon. It was only typical that Carolyn came with him. Maggie and I followed the church and our friend. It didn't turn out so bad after all."

"Oh," Oliver said. "That's nice of you. What were you doing in your previous town?"

"Nothing important," Leticia said and scratched her neck. "I was a waitress too after the war. The war took its toll on me and it's too traumatic to talk about. I just want to put the past behind me."

Oliver squeezed her hand. "I understand. Completely."

Now Leticia was feeling very vulnerable. Oliver's gaze was unyielding. He kept his eyes on hers with a faint smile on his face. She felt the heat rise in her throat as she lowered her eyes and let her gaze drop to his lips. She instinctively bit hers. Something was pushing her to do it. All she had to do was lean in. Slowly... slow enough that Oliver had time to react and decide if he wanted this.

But Oliver went in for the kiss before her head even moved more than two inches. He cupped her cheek in his palm and planted a kiss on her lips. Leticia held her breath as the fireworks went off in her head. She melted into his arms, completely certain that she had fallen for Oliver in a big and irreversible way.

Guilt fought with her feelings; would he be so happy if he knew she was a saloon girl?

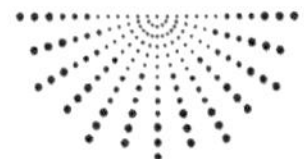

CHAPTER SIX

"I'm sure, Dad," Sam said. "They might actually be in danger and I'm worried."

Oliver was listening, and he shared her worry, but his mind was split. On one hand, he was attentively listening to Samantha talk about Edwin learning Braille, and on the other hand, he was replaying the events of the night before in his head. The kiss with Leticia, their long talk, the drive back to the restaurant, holding hands. There was no doubt that he was starting to feel something close to new love. Something he had not felt in years.

Who could blame him? Leticia was gorgeous. She had emerald green eyes that gazed at him so inquisitively, a smile that could brighten a dark day, and there was a way she talked that kept him interested. So bold, so outspoken... Leticia was a kindred spirit.

"Dad? Dad, are you listening?" Samantha asked and waved her hand in the air in front of him.

Oliver snapped out of his thoughts and looked at her. "Yes. I'll get in touch with someone I know, and inquire about Edwin learning braille. I think we should start with the books you were able to acquire. Margaret can read them to him. In fact, I actually think we should include Margaret in the learning process."

Samantha slapped her palm to her forehead and sighed. "We have already agreed on that, Dad. We were talking about Leticia and her friends, and how I think they are in danger."

Danger! "Oh, sorry. I was distracted," Oliver said.

"By what?" Sam asked, her right eyebrow was raised, she was teasing him.

"You don't want to know. Now, where were we?"

"Did you ask Leticia about her past? Where they came from or why they came to Appleton?"

"I did, but she said they followed Sherman. They followed the church, Sam. I think that's the obvious answer."

Samantha sat on the desk. "I don't think so."

"Why not? Why are you so sure that they are in danger?" The word sent a shock through him and made him want to get up and go see Leticia, but he kept his face and body neutral. He was not ready for Sam to know his feelings and was sure that she was overreacting.

"I'm not completely sure that they are in danger, I'm saying that I think so because of what I heard. I told you. I went to the restaurant to visit Maggie and her friends, and I overheard one of them say that their life was going well and they were happy at last. The person hoped that they stayed happy and that the events of their past didn't come back to haunt them. It's not just that, Dad. When Edwin realized he was going blind, I heard them say some questionable things too, referencing their past. I really want to know what that past is, and if they are still in danger. I want to help, Dad."

"I know, honey, but it doesn't seem like they need any help," Oliver said. "But it is pretty suspicious, and I see where you're coming from. For now, focus on caring for Edwin and his sight. I'll get to the bottom of it."

"What do you plan on doing?" Samantha asked.

"I should go to the source. Sherman is the one who can answer our questions honestly, isn't he? He's the town's preacher, and he knows them well. He might be able to tell me something about Leticia's past."

"All right then," Samantha said. "When do you plan on going?"

"Right now. I'll just stop by the church to meet with Sherman before I go to Darby's house for his weekly checkup."

"Tell me whatever it is you find out."

"I will. I would hate for the curiosity to kill you, Sam."

Samantha rolled her eyes and rose from the table. Once Oliver threw his coat on, he made his way out of the house. It was quite windy that afternoon, and he had a lot of work to get done, but going to the church seemed like the most important thing.

Samantha had every right to be worried. Oliver recalled how stiff Leticia got when he mentioned her past. It took her a minute before she was able to look him directly in the eye again, and he could feel her hand tremble when he placed his on hers. There had to be a story there, and Oliver wanted to find out what it was.

On reaching the church, Oliver went straight for Sherman's office. He wasn't sure the town's preacher was going to be in there working. The man was always active, going around the town, and helping people. Oliver admired his wit and selflessness. He loved it when people didn't hesitate to help.

After taking a second to gather himself, Oliver rapped on the door softly. "Pastor Sherman? It's Oliver Randall."

"Doctor Randall, do come in," Sherman said.

Relieved that his journey had not been in vain, Sherman twisted the door knob and walked into the room. He met Sherman standing with a warm smile on his face.

"Good afternoon, Pastor Sherman," Oliver greeted, approaching the desk.

"What a pleasant surprise. I wasn't expecting to see you today, Doctor Randall."

"Oh, I was hoping to speak to you about a matter that has been on my mind for a while," Oliver said. "Do you mind if I sit?"

"Not at all, please do," Sherman said and took his seat too. "Ask me anything. I'm more than happy to help. I trust all is well at the clinic?"

"All is well," Oliver answered. "The clinic isn't why I'm here. I'm actually here to talk about you. First off, I would like to say that you and the church have been doing an amazingly good job in the town. Everyone loves you and you've done so much for the community since you arrived. It's really admirable."

Sherman interlocked his fingers on the table and lowered his head. "It's nothing to thank me for, Doctor Randall. My parishioners and I see Appleton as our home now. The community has been nothing but welcoming."

"I'm glad to hear that. It'll be a shame if you were planning on leaving," Oliver said and leaned forward. "But I am curious. I do want to know the journey that brought you here. What drew you and your parishioners to Appleton? I mean, there has to be a story. How did you reach this point? I'd like to hear it."

Sherman's eyes dimmed and he leaned back. He cleared his throat and tried to smile again, but Oliver could see that he was forcing it.

"That's a long story, like most people, but I think that what we should be focused on now, is the future and what it holds. Not the past and its stories."

Oliver stifled a sigh of frustration. He was beating around the bush, the same thing he did with Leticia. It was obvious at this point that there was something. Was Samantha right and the group was truly in danger? Was Leticia in danger?

"So, Doctor Randall..."

"Pastor Sherman, hang on," Oliver said, cutting him off. "I am just going to come out and say it. I don't want to beat around the bush anymore. Samantha has heard things. Not rumors, or hearsays, but things that Leticia, Carolyn, and Margaret have said. She is convinced that there's a story here, and I'm convinced too. Something happened, something drove you to South Dakota?"

Sherman's smile waned. "Doctor Randall, I don't know what you're thinking, but whatever it is, it's wrong. Now, it's our past, not yours. And if it doesn't affect anyone, I don't see any reason to bring it up."

"Please don't get me wrong. I am not here to judge, Pastor Sherman. I would never do that," Oliver said.

"I didn't say you were judging."

"I just want to know if you're in danger or something of the sort. That's what we think, and that's why we're worried."

Sherman squinted his eyes. "Are you worried that we are a threat to the community? Because if that's what you're implying-"

"It's definitely not what I'm implying."

"Then what are you implying?"

Oliver took in a deep breath and mellowed. Sherman was reading meaning into his suspicion and he didn't like it one bit. Oliver had to make him see that he had no ill intentions toward them. Perhaps that way, they'd trust him.

"I like Leticia," Oliver announced. "I'm courting her, and I think my feelings for her are getting stronger by the day. But it bothers me that she might be in danger. Samantha heard them speak, and she was bothered too. This is the first time Samantha has actually made such close friends. She usually prefers to be alone. She's worried, and I'm worried. I just want to know that there's nothing to worry about and to do that, I need to know why Leticia came to Appleton. Please."

Sherman studied him for a brief moment in silence before he cleared his throat again. "I can tell you, but you'd have to promise to keep it to yourself. Carolyn and her friends have come a long way. You cannot ruin this for them."

"I will."

"I know you, Doctor and I know of your reputation. That's why I'm choosing to trust you. Do I have your word, Doctor Randall?"

"You do," Oliver said, leaning forward.

"I'll be brief," Sherman started. "Carolyn, Leticia, and Margaret followed the church to South Dakota because they had to run for their lives."

Oliver's heart skipped a beat. "Oh, dear Lord."

"It started when they journeyed to the West in search of security and happiness. They were innocent, and they wanted to find love and be happy together. But their innocence led them into the wrong hands. A man called Porter took advantage of their naivety and lied to them. He told them that he could get them good husbands, if they came west." Sherman paused to see that Oliver was following.

"I don't like the sound of this, those poor ladies."

"They believed him, and they came west, to Minnesota. Porter was the one who paid for their train tickets, and when they got there, he demanded they pay him back even though he didn't match them with their husbands."

"But, what man wouldn't want such wonderful wives?"

"It was a con he pulled regularly. The women had to work in a saloon, serving drinks. Normally, he would wait until they were broken and then marry them off for money to some horrible brute. Carolyn was forced into a sham marriage to a vile man to help Leticia and Margaret escape. But in the end, the three of them managed to escape, and together with me and a few parishioners, we set off to search for a new place to live. Porter caught up with us and tried to forcefully take them all back to Minnesota at gunpoint. He held Leticia and he threatened to kill her if they didn't do his bidding. Leticia was the one who saved them all. She took the gun from Porter, disarming him, and she was able to scare them off with it. That's how we escaped and after some journey, we settled here in South Dakota."

Oliver was dumbfounded. He stared at Sherman, unable to believe his ears. Leticia had held a gun... to a man's head? She had gone through all of that.

"Oliver, I trust you to keep this to yourself."

Oliver nodded and sat up, still visibly confused. "I will."

"And now you know the facts of the matter, I'm sure a lot is going through your mind. Leticia worked in a saloon, she ran away, she held a gun... you're thinking of all of that and it's overwhelming. But I want you to think long and hard about what it is that you want. If it's too much for you to take in, I'd advise you to take a step back now from Leticia. The ladies are still pretty shaken by it all, and the last thing I want is for Leticia's heart to be broken again. Take a step back, and think about it before you approach her again. She has suffered too much heartbreak."

"I understand where you're coming from," Oliver said. "I will do nothing to interfere with their newfound happiness. Leticia told me that she loved this town. The last thing I want to do is make it hard for her to live here."

"Thank you," Sherman said.

Oliver thanked Sherman and rose to his feet. Sherman had given him a rundown of everything, and yet Oliver was sure that they could expand on that past for hours. What did Leticia do at the saloon? How did they escape? What did Leticia do with the gun? Did she still have it? There was so much to think about that Oliver felt his feelings waiver for the first time.

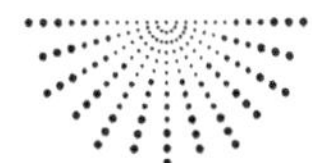

CHAPTER SEVEN

It was getting difficult for Leticia to steal glances at Oliver. Not only was he starting to notice, but Samantha had caught her gaze twice. Leticia wondered if Oliver had told his daughter about their relationship. Did it mean she was expected to inform Carolyn and Margaret too? In her mind, it was still too fresh to be spreading the news.

But they had shared a kiss, and Leticia didn't think it was too soon for that. Plus, she had to admit that if Oliver told Samantha about her, then it was actually flattering. It would mean that he was serious if he had decided to inform his daughter, wouldn't it? Serious enough to tell the closest person to him. Perhaps it was time for her to speak to her friends too. They had been waiting for such news for the longest time. Carolyn and Margaret were bound to have noticed something by now.

"You are hiding something from me, Leticia Baker," Carolyn said, appearing in front of her and blocking her view of the handsome doctor. She crossed her arms and tilted her head to the side. "Either that or I'm over-thinking things because we aren't together all of the time like we used to be."

Leticia opened her mouth to speak but the words refused to form. "You're overthinking things," she managed to say. "Why are you staring at me like that?"

"Because I am furious with you," Carolyn said, poking Leticia on the arm. "Why did you leave me all alone in the kitchen? Do you really want me to fry all of that chicken by myself? Penny was kind enough to let us host the dinner here at the restaurant, but she had plans for the evening, so it's just the two of us that are doing all the work. But what do you do? You abandon me."

Leticia gasped. She had actually forgotten that she was working in the kitchen. Her plan had been to slip out and peek to see if Oliver had arrived, but when she saw him, her mind went completely blank. Things could have been a lot worse if Carolyn wasn't in the kitchen. Leticia had left the chicken to fry, and she had been out here for about twenty minutes.

"Oh, goodness. I put some chicken on the stove."

"You did, and you left it. But I looked after it," Carolyn said. "Now, can we please go back into the kitchen and finish preparing the dinner so we can get the show on the road? Edwin is really nervous."

"Right, sorry. Let's go." They walked back to the kitchen and immediately set about finishing the meal. They worked so well together that it was as if they knew what the other person was thinking.

"What did you come out to do anyways?" Carolyn asked, walking in front of her.

"I came to check on the guests. It seems all of them have arrived," Leticia answered.

"Not all of them. Sherman isn't here yet," Carolyn said, walking into the kitchen. "I wonder why he's taking so long. Everyone else is here."

"He will be here," Leticia assured her. "You know he will. Besides, preparation for the wedding has to be tiring and he insists on doing most of the heavy work. I can't wait for your wedding day to come, Carolyn."

Carolyn shrieked excitedly. "Me too. Everything seems to be going so smoothly and the day is drawing closer. To think that right after my wedding, we will have to start planning Margaret's wedding. Isn't it exciting?"

Leticia gave Carolyn a funny look. "What if tonight, Maggie shocks us all and says she's not ready to get married? What do you think is going to happen?"

"That's not going to happen, Letty. You know it. I actually think that Margaret is even more excited to marry Edwin than Edwin is to marry her."

"I doubt it." Leticia shook her head. "No. Edwin fell in love with Margaret the first time he laid eyes on her. There's no way Maggie loves him more than he loves her. No way at all. It's like saying you are more excited to marry Sherman than Sherman is to marry you. It's absurd. We are not blind."

Carolyn stopped massaging the spices into the chicken and turned to Leticia. "I wonder when someone will come to us and confess that they are in love with you, Letty. Don't you think that day will be magical?"

Leticia scoffed and threw bread crumbs at Carolyn. "Not to worry. You will be shocked. You can count on it."

"Really? Because that's all I'm hoping for. You know how fulfilled we would all feel when we achieve our dreams of falling in love and starting a family? Can you imagine it? Think far into the future. The three of us gathered outside, complaining about how our kids are keeping us up all through the night?"

Leticia smiled and saw the same future Carolyn was imagining. "It'll happen. We don't need to imagine it. It's our future."

They smiled at each other. In no time, dinner was ready and served. Once Carolyn and Leticia had confirmed that everything was set, they freshened up and returned to the table. Leticia sat by Carolyn's side, with Oliver across the table, two seats to the right. Edwin headed the table, while Margaret sat to his left. Just as they were about to begin, Sherman hurried into the room. He greeted everyone, placed a peck on Carolyn's forehead, and sat by her side.

"I apologize for being late," Sherman said. "I had some business to take care of and I didn't anticipate that it was going to take this long."

Carolyn tapped his hand. "It's all right. We were just about to begin."

Half an hour into the dinner, Carolyn nudged Leticia on the side and gestured to Edwin and Margaret. They exchanged knowing looks and watched the couple whisper and giggle to each other.

"Edwin never leaves Maggie's side," Carolyn whispered to Leticia.

Leticia leaned in. "You mean Maggie never leaves Edwin's side?"

"Must you always argue my point?"

"I'm not arguing, I'm just saying. I think it's the opposite. Maggie's the one who never leaves his side. Do you remember it was Edwin's idea to get the cane? If it was left to Maggie, she'd be his cane."

Carolyn giggled. "You're right. But I love the fact that Edwin's learning braille. It's a brilliant idea."

"I know. Plus, yesterday, I saw him strolling down the street on my way to the market. I asked him if Maggie knew he was outside, you know, because Maggie was back at the restaurant, but he said she didn't know. He was trying to make his way around all by himself. I tried to help, but he declined. He even told me exactly where he was. Apparently, he and Maggie have learned to count steps, so he knows how many houses he was away from his home."

Carolyn stared at Margaret then turned back to Leticia. "I'm so happy for them. Maggie is the most encouraging person I know. She's perfect for him."

Leticia saw Edwin interlock his fingers on the table and clear his throat simultaneously. She gasped and nudged Carolyn.

"That's our cue. Give him the wine."

Carolyn gasped too and quickly filled a glass with white wine. She passed it to Sherman who then pressed it into Edwin's hand. A wide smile formed on Edwin's face the same time a confused look formed on Margaret's.

Edwin clinked his glass and rose to his feet. "If I may have everyone's attention, please?"

The small table of close friends stopped the side chattering and turned their gaze on him. Leticia briefly glanced at Oliver and smiled at him. He smiled back, but the smile didn't appear to reach his eyes.

"Thank you," Edwin continued. "First, I'd like to thank everyone for coming tonight. It means a lot to me. This moment right here is precious to me. After I got the news of my blindness, I never thought this day would come. For that, I'm thankful. I'm thankful for life, friends, and my soul mate. Margaret... Maggie, I wish I could still see you. I've come to terms with being blind and unable to see the world, but I am not fine without seeing you. If I could see only you, just you alone, that would be something. I don't know if this makes any sense, but I feel your love. Everywhere. In your words, in your actions, when you constantly trail me everywhere I go, when you gasp every time I try to do anything myself. I love you, and I would not trade you for the world. Honestly, I strongly believe that I was a hero in my former life. I think I saved the world. If not, how else do I explain what I did to deserve you, Maggie?"

"Oh, Edwin. You and your words." Margaret giggled. "I love you too. Thank you."

Sherman rose to his feet and pulled out a small, blue box. He placed it in Edwin's hands and pushed the chair away to give Edwin room to get down on one knee. Edwin opened the box to reveal a ring.

"Maggie..." he started.

Margaret gasped and rose to her feet.

"Please make me the happiest man in the world and marry me. I promise to make you happy for as long as I shall live. I will do everything possible to be a husband to you, not a burden. I will learn braille; I will master it to the point where I can teach at that school for the blind that Samantha told us about yesterday. I will make sure to get in touch with Albert Morris, the owner, and learn from him too. Maggie, I will be the best husband that I can be for you. Please, say yes."

Margaret began to cry and for a minute Leticia worried that her naïve friend was going to make a spontaneous, surprising decision.

"Edwin, you didn't have to say too much. You already owned my heart from the very first day we met in that wagon. I will marry you. Yes. I have no doubt in my heart."

Everyone stood to their feet and applauded loudly as Margaret helped Edwin to his feet. They wrapped their arms around each other and rocked from side to side. Leticia sighed in relief and hugged Carolyn too. She was on the verge of tears and at that moment, she turned to Oliver. In response, Oliver looked away, his gaze hard, his expression unsmiling.

Leticia could swear that her heart paused when she saw him avert his eyes.

"Oh, what now?" she whispered.

CHAPTER EIGHT

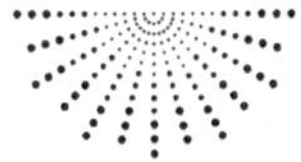

"Ou both knew, didn't you? That's why you planned all of this?" Margaret asked, accosting her friends in the corner.

As much as Leticia wanted to show Margaret just how happy she was for her, she couldn't. Not when she was so worried about Oliver's sudden change in demeanor. There wasn't much to think about. Something had happened. It was one of two things. He had lost interest, or he had found something out.

If it was the former... "No," Leticia whispered.

It couldn't be the former. What in the world could have made him lose interest in her in the space of three days? The latter was more apt to explain the sudden change in his demeanor. Oliver must have heard something about her that had caused him to lose interest. But what exactly did he hear? And from who?

"Letty!" Margaret said, hugging her. "What's wrong? You look pale."

Leticia forced a smile. "I was just thinking, that's all. I'm happy for you, Maggie. You get the happy ending that you deserve with Edwin."

"Thank you, Letty. I still can't believe you both kept this from me. We work together all the time, and you did this. So cruel." She wagged her finger in mock admonishment but the huge smile on her face denied her words.

"We were sneaking around so much that Leticia was sure you had found out," Carolyn said. "That day you walked into the kitchen while we were discussing the type of ring Edwin was going to use to propose."

"I didn't know," Margaret responded. "You both told me the dinner was for Edwin to cheer him up and give him the strength he needs to pursue his dreams. You lied to me."

"Technically, we didn't lie. The dinner was for Edwin to cheer him on and give him the opportunity he needed to pursue his dreams. Which in this case is marrying you. No lies were told."

Carolyn and Margaret laughed at Leticia's statement, but Leticia didn't find it funny. She couldn't find anything funny, not when Oliver was giving her the silent treatment. He was nowhere in sight, but Leticia was positive that he had not left. His coat was with Samantha, and Samantha was still there so that meant he was around somewhere. Just out of her sight.

"Anyway, thank you both," Margaret continued. "Thank you so much for this surprise. I knew Edwin was going to propose, but I didn't think he was going to do it like this. I reckoned he'd ask me at home, early in the morning, before I headed out to work. I'd most likely be in the kitchen making breakfast."

Leticia arched her eyebrows. "That's pretty specific."

"Trust me. I've imagined it countless times. But this... this was wonderful and I did not see it coming."

"He wanted everyone to know just how much he loves you," Carolyn said. "I'm happy for you, honey. I was just telling Leticia that after my wedding, we have to start making preparations for yours."

"Thankfully, yours will be the blueprint. I'll just do whatever you do." Margaret shrugged her shoulders. "Oh, today is the happiest day of my entire life. I feel on top of the world."

Today was one of the most disappointing days of Leticia's life. She felt like the world she built was crumbling down. Oliver was slowly shattering the hope she had held on to so dearly, the little optimism she had summoned. What in the world went wrong? Now she understood why Oliver had not said a word to her since he arrived. Leticia expected him to walk up to her long before the dinner even commenced, but he didn't. She should have seen that red flag first.

Perhaps, she could ask Samantha why Oliver was avoiding her. But she now had a firm suspicion that Oliver and Samantha were onto something. What if Samantha knew? What if she was aware of the reason Oliver had refused to hold her stare?

"Leticia? Is there something you want to tell us?" Margaret asked.

Leticia snapped back to reality. "What? Why would you assume that?"

"Because you've been quiet for a while, and you, my friend... you are only quiet when you're thinking about something. What's on your mind?"

"Nothing," Leticia lied. "Just random things. Please give me a minute, I'll be right back. One moment."

Leticia had changed her mind. Instead of going to Samantha, she was going to find Oliver and confront him herself. That was the best way to handle the situation, by taking the bull by its horns. If Oliver had an issue with her, or if he had heard something and had chosen to believe it, then he needed to say it to her face. Leticia held high hopes for the evening. She had even asked for the fiddlers to be hired for the evening, so she and Oliver could dance.

"Maybe I'm overthinking this," she whispered, walking out of the restaurant. "Maybe I am. Let's just talk to him before jumping to any conclusions."

Leticia tried to be optimistic as she searched for Oliver outside the restaurant. She wanted to believe that it was all in her head, that it was her overthinking, but deep down, she knew it was not. She had seen Oliver's face. He looked guilty about something, and if she had to guess what it was, Leticia would guess that Oliver felt guilty for leading her on. Her only issue was figuring out what it was that changed his mind.

"Oliver?" Leticia called out to him, walking by the white elm trees on the other side of the road.

With no sign of him, she started to panic, but she managed to keep her nerves under control. It wasn't the first time her heart had been shattered by love, hence, she could manage her emotions well. But one thing she couldn't do was let the doubts and questions linger. She was willing to go all the way to the clinic if she had to.

"Oliver?" Leticia said and sighed in relief. He stood with his back against a tree, his gaze set on the ground.

With her heart in her mouth, Leticia walked up to him and stood by his side. It was a full moon that night, and his face shone subtly in the moonlight. She could see that he was troubled. She was right. There was a problem.

"Why did you leave the party?" Leticia asked him. "You haven't had dessert yet. It's cake. Carolyn and I made it."

Oliver kept his gaze on the ground. "Thank you, but I'm not really hungry."

"Oh, is something wrong? Is something bothering you?"

Oliver sighed and ran his fingers through his hair. "No, nothing's bothering me. How are you, Leticia?"

Even a child could lie better than Oliver. "I'm all right. How are you?"

"I'm all right too," he said, unenthusiastically.

Leticia took in a deep breath and scanned the path. "It's a bit cold out today. Would you prefer to go inside? I really think you should have some cake. Plus, the fiddlers have arrived, and they are already playing. You said you wanted us to dance again, and this is a perfect opportunity to do so, don't you think? It's a lovely evening, everyone is happy. Everyone except you..."

Oliver lifted his head. "Oh, I'm happy. I'm really happy for Margaret and Edwin. They deserve to be happy together."

"Oh. So, why won't you look at me?" Leticia asked. "Something is wrong, isn't it?"

Oliver stood upright. "I'm fine, Leticia. Let's go inside."

Oh, there was that feeling in the pit of her stomach. Leticia could sense it. She could sense his confusion, his doubt, his darting questioning gaze. Oliver knew something. She couldn't forget his inquiry into her past when they had gone to the creek days ago. Was that what it was about? Her past? Oliver had no problems with her when she told him about her past love. So, it wasn't about Dwight. But he had been curious about where she was coming from and what she did. Perhaps, someone had told him?

"Something is wrong, isn't it?" Leticia asked, crossing her arms. "What is it? Tell me. I want to hear it."

Oliver shook his head. "Nothing is wrong. I just needed some fresh air, that's all."

"You have not looked at me for more than a second tonight," Leticia said. "And you know why I find that strange? You had no problem holding my gaze before. What changed? Tell me what it is."

"It's nothing," Oliver said.

Leticia drew in a deep breath, preparing herself for the bold declaration she was about to make. She stood in front of Oliver, blocking his path. Leticia fixed her eyes on his face and exhaled.

"I was a saloon girl before I came here to Appleton."

There it was. The confirmation. Oliver didn't flinch. He knew. There was no shock, no vivid expression on his face, no concern, no confusion, nothing. All he did was shut his eyes and sigh. Leticia's blood chilled.

"Leticia…"

"How did you find out?" she asked. "How did you come to learn about my past? Who did you ask? You went around, asking people about me, didn't you? You know everything."

Oliver met her gaze and took a step closer. "It doesn't matter. I…"

The words seemed to have caught in Oliver's throat. It was then Leticia realized that he had grown distant. She should have known when he didn't seek her out for three whole days after their time together.

"You could have said something," Leticia said softly.

"I was going to," Oliver answered.

"No, you weren't. You were going to keep avoiding me," Leticia retorted. "But it's all right. I understand your decision."

"What?" Oliver asked. "Let me…"

"I don't think you need to say anymore, Doctor Randall. I understand. You've heard everything about me, and you no longer wish to court me anymore. I get that, and honestly, I knew it was coming. I would have just preferred that you told me, instead of keeping me in the dark and ignoring me."

Oliver took a step closer and reached for her. "Let me say something, Leticia. I wasn't trying to..."

She took a step back in response and put up her hands in front of him. "I don't need an explanation, Doctor Randall. You don't have to feel guilty about having doubts. Everyone has them. Let's just be civil about this. It's easier this way."

"No, it's not. Leticia, you're not listening to me."

"It just wasn't meant to be, I guess. Goodbye, Oliver."

With that, Leticia hurried back into the restaurant, trying to keep her emotions under control. It was better to cut her losses then and there. Her heart was too fragile for anything intense. She couldn't listen to Oliver's words, or hear him publicly declare that he didn't want to court her anymore. It was easier when she did it. Heartbreaking, but easier.

CHAPTER NINE

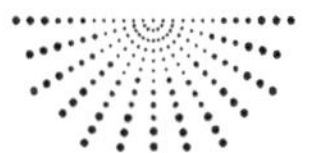

It was the perfect day, for the perfect wedding. The sun was out in a glorious display high in the sky, but its rays weren't as harsh. Leticia had been worried two days ago because it had rained heavily. She didn't want rain for Carolyn's special day.

Thankfully, the sun had shone for two days straight, drying up the muddy path. It was a beautiful day that they had all been anticipating for a while. However, Leticia had to fight the urge to cry. Her emotions were all over the place and she didn't want to spoil things for her friends.

The ceremony had been beautiful. Carolyn walked down the aisle, cued in by the wedding tune. Leticia caught the proud look on Sherman's face as he watched her walk up to him with a bouquet of wild roses in her hands.

Her wedding gown had a square-cut neck and long sleeves. It swept the ground as she walked. The veil over her face did very little to mask Carolyn's beauty. Leticia could see her beaming from where she sat.

Edwin presided over the ceremony. He had been made a deacon the week before at the church, and Margaret talked about how he worked day and night, learning braille to impress people at the ceremony. Edwin did a remarkable job. He read the vows and the Bible verses partly in braille, and partly from memory. All the while, Margaret watched him with clenched fists. Watching Margaret amused Leticia. She could not be more obvious about her feelings.

"I now pronounce you, man and wife," Edwin said out loud. "You may kiss the bride."

Leticia and Margaret held hands together and shrieked like little girls when Sherman reached for Carolyn and lifted her veil. He placed both hands on her cheeks gently and kissed her on her lips. Carolyn responded by grabbing Sherman by the waist. The congregation cheered for them and kept cheering until they began to walk down the aisle.

"Letty, do you think we made enough chicken?" Margaret asked as they made their way to the kitchen behind the church. "I don't think we made enough chicken."

"Oh, Maggie. You're just being paranoid," Leticia told her. "The chicken is more than enough. We prepared more than enough. It'll go round, trust me."

Margaret nodded. "Oh, I know, it's just that they finally did it. I feel so relieved. Do you recall how worried Carolyn was when we first moved here to Appleton? Remember how she kept worrying that she wasn't good enough to be a wife to Sherman?"

Leticia smiled. "Thankfully, she didn't let the worrying ruin things for her and Sherman. See how good they look together. Is it just me that simply cannot imagine Carolyn with anyone else?"

"Nope. Sherman is her soulmate, and I am so happy for her. If they had not met, I wonder where we would be right now."

Leticia shuddered. "I dare not think about it. We're slowly achieving our dreams, Maggie. We're doing it."

She smiled brightly even though her heart was breaking. She would not ruin things for her two best friends.

At least Margaret and Carolyn were doing it. Leticia on the other hand was back to square one. To make matters even worse, she not only went back to the starting point, but she had also developed strong feelings for Oliver that kept her up at night. She wanted to tell Carolyn and Margaret about her brief courtship with Oliver so badly, but it wasn't the right time. Not with all the excitement they were feeling. So, she kept it to herself. It was depressing, and sometimes, she wondered if things could have gone differently. She was also curious as to how Oliver found out, and why he was that interested in her past.

The wedding reception followed almost immediately. They were all gathered in the yard in the church, both the parishioners and the townsfolk. Leticia could see why Margaret had been so worried. It seemed like Sherman had invited the entire community. But they had prepared adequately for it, hence they had nothing to worry about. Everything had to be perfect for Carolyn. It was a once-in-a-lifetime experience and they wanted it to be full of good memories.

They had invited the fiddlers again to play at the event. Leticia moved her head from side to side, loving the music that they made. She wanted to dance, but she chose not to. Everyone else was dancing. Carolyn and Sherman danced in each other's arms, whispering, Margaret and Edwin danced too, also whispering. Margaret had a habit of reporting everything she could see to Edwin. She would describe things to him, tell him what everyone else was doing, and what the scenery looked like. When Margaret turned to stare at Leticia, Leticia knew she was telling Edwin how she was sitting alone with a glass of wine in her hand. Margaret blew a raspberry at Leticia, causing her to scoff.

"When will I escape from this taunting?" Leticia murmured, downing the contents of her glass.

"Doctor Randall," Edwin said, turning to his side. Margaret handed him his cane and guided him forward.

A frown formed on Leticia's face as she turned around to find Oliver seated just a few feet from her. She gasped and turned back around, embarrassed. How did she not notice that he was there? So close to her? How long had he been sitting there?

"Yes, Edwin?" Oliver said, rising to his feet.

"I was wondering. You have no one to dance with, and Leticia here has no one to dance with either. How about you both share a dance? I mean, there's no harm in sharing a dance with someone you're acquainted with."

Leticia held her breath and turned to stare at Oliver. She froze, unable to think or figure a way out of the awkward predicament. Of all the people gathered there at the reception, Edwin had to ask Oliver. There was no way they knew of their relationship – or rather, of their former relationship.

"Uh, Edwin," Leticia said breathlessly, trying to save Oliver from the embarrassment.

Leticia dug her fingers into her palm. Deep down, she secretly hoped that Oliver would agree to the dance. They had not seen each other in almost two weeks. After their conversation at the engagement dinner, Leticia refused to go to town. Carolyn and Margaret simply thought she was bored of it, but she was trying to avoid the doctor at every cost. Oliver usually came to the restaurant for lunch, but he had stopped coming. They had not seen each other in days, and it hurt Leticia because she missed him so dearly. Why did he have to go digging around into her past?

"I'm too tired to dance," Oliver said, sitting back down. "But thank you for the suggestion. I think I prefer watching you all enjoy yourselves."

Edwin shrugged his shoulders. "All right. If that's what you want to do."

With the help of his cane and Margaret's arm, Edwin walked over to Leticia's side and stopped in front of her. He sat down and placed his cane in between his legs.

"You shouldn't have done that, Edwin," Leticia said, slapping his arm. "Now you have made things awkward."

"Why? I thought you and the doctor were friends. Friends dance with each other, don't they? And you both danced together the last time so I didn't see a problem."

"Well, I don't want to dance," Leticia lied. "You didn't have to do that."

"Maggie asked me to," Edwin replied. "She didn't like seeing you sit alone, so she asked me to get Doctor Randall to dance with you."

"Well, that was sweet, but I'm fine," Leticia said. "I'm not in the mood to dance. But I appreciate the concern."

"Do you want to dance with me?" Margaret asked. "Come on, I know how much you like to dance."

"Maggie, it's all right," Leticia said, forcing a smile. "You don't have to look out for me. Seriously, I'd prefer to sit here and watch you."

Margaret sighed, reluctant to budge. "Well, all right then. But if you feel like dancing, you know where to find us."

"I do," Leticia said.

When they stood up and left, Leticia sprang to her feet too. She was embarrassed, to say the least. It was the second time Oliver had rejected her and being around him was causing her heart to flutter. Ignoring him, she made her way out of the yard, fighting so hard to keep a smile on her face so people didn't suspect that she was on the verge of tears. She moved to the other side of the street and stood behind a tree.

Porter Hathaway had managed to ruin things for her once again. Leticia slid down to the ground, exhausted and tired of hiding everything. The mere thought that Oliver had heard about her working at the saloon, enduring all that embarrassment, or that he had heard about her threatening a man with a gun, made Leticia cringe. It was a shame she had tried so hard to hide. Carolyn and Margaret had convinced her that it was nothing to be worried about, because she saved their lives, but apparently, it mattered to people.

If Oliver knew, then who else? Did Samantha know? Who else knew that they worked at a saloon before they came to Appleton? If it got out, then what Carolyn feared the most was going to happen. People were going to question her suitability to be a wife to Sherman, regardless of the truth.

But the most painful thing for Leticia was losing Oliver. Losing love again. It was too much. She was so tired and she never wanted to wear her heart on her sleeve again. Perhaps love just wasn't for her. There were people like that, and she must be one of them.

CHAPTER TEN

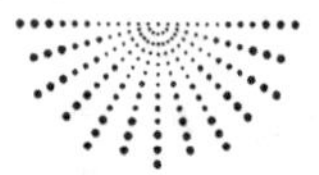

"What are you doing?"

"What do you mean?" Oliver asked Samantha, snapping out of his thoughts. Should he have just said yes to the dance?

Oliver rubbed his face with his palms roughly and sighed. The past few days had been difficult for him, almost too much for him to handle. He was filled with regret. He had taken a drink of whiskey, twice. Tending to his patients was difficult because he kept thinking about Leticia and got distracted every five minutes. Sam had practically been the one running the clinic in his stead. He trusted her to handle things, while he took his time torturing himself for not stopping Leticia from leaving with the wrong impression of him.

The news of Leticia's past had worried him, very much, too much, Oliver had to admit. But that had been it. He was skeptical, and he had many questions. There were blank spaces in Sherman's story, and Oliver had been too dumbfounded that day to ask them. Why was working at a saloon their only option? What did Leticia do at the saloon, or what was so bad about working there that she had to run for her life? Were they still being chased? Was that why Margaret was paranoid like Samantha had said? Was he sure he wanted to get involved in the situation?

So many thoughts had been running through his mind that night that he had acted badly. He couldn't stop himself from overthinking the situation, and when Leticia confronted him, he still was confused. But Oliver never intended on ending their relationship. He just needed space to wrap his head around Leticia's story. His intention was never to stop courting her.

To make matters worse, he didn't stop her that night, and he let her think whatever she wanted to. Oliver couldn't help but imagine how much she hated him now for what he did. Sherman had warned him about breaking Leticia's heart but he went on and did exactly that.

"Dad?" Sam called him. "Would you snap out of it?"

"Snap of out what?"

"Feeling sorry for yourself," Sam explained. "You are ruining your chances of a fresh start. Three days ago, in your drunken state, you told me that you were falling in love with Leticia. Why do you then choose to torture yourself this way? It's simple."

"It's not, Sam," Oliver answered. "It's not that simple. I might like Leticia very much, yes. But it still doesn't change the fact that I don't know enough about her."

"Then get to know her," Sam insisted. "Make the choice yourself and talk to her."

"It's not that easy, Sam."

Sam placed her hand on Oliver's shoulder. "Now I feel guilty because I'm the one that asked you to find out about their past. I have peace of mind now, knowing that they are far from their troubles, but I hate seeing you like this."

"It's not your fault. I was bound to find out anyway." He shrugged.

"Dad, the past is just that. It's the past. You cannot change it, but you surely can learn from it. What Leticia needs from you right now is assurance. She doesn't deserve to be judged by her past."

"I'm not judging," Oliver said.

"Good, then go and find her. Talk to her."

"Sam, let me handle it. I'll take care of it. You don't need to concern yourself with this."

"Yes, I do. I already told you. I feel responsible for this misunderstanding, and I would appreciate it if you fixed it. Or would you prefer that I speak to Letty on your behalf?"

"No," Oliver said without hesitation. "I'll do it myself."

"Good. Go do it, now."

"I'm going."

Oliver shook his head and stood up from the chair. He had no idea where Leticia was, but Samantha was right. He needed to find her. It was his fault that she had left the celebration, and he felt bad keeping her away from her friends on such a special day. He was ruining it for her. Such knowledge crushed his heart and he felt queasy. What had he done?

Oliver didn't know what he wanted to say to Leticia just yet, or how he was going to win her back. All that was important, was bringing her back to the party before her friends noticed that she had disappeared.

After about ten minutes of walking, Oliver had not caught a glimpse of her. He was starting to worry. She couldn't have strayed that far from the party. Unless she went to a specific place.

Oliver stopped to think. He had walked in circles for a while, but Leticia wasn't anywhere to be seen. It was either she went to the restaurant, or she went home. Those options were unlikely. The restaurant was in the opposite direction from where a parishioner had said he saw Leticia. If she was walking down the path, then she was headed to the edge of the town.

"The creek," Oliver said and snapped his fingers.

It had to be it. Oliver gazed at the sky, noticing how nice the weather was. If Leticia wanted to be alone, she would go somewhere peaceful, somewhere she had only recently fallen in love with.

With that in mind, he made his way to the creek. He felt good inside, knowing that Leticia did not have a problem going to the creek, where they had shared a kiss.

Thinking of it made him smile. He wondered if it was possible to fix their relationship. The almost two weeks he spent apart from Leticia confirmed to him just how much she meant to him and just how much he loved her.

Was it too late to get her back?

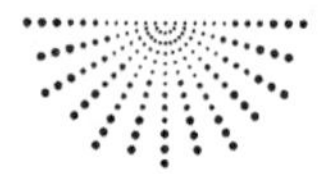

CHAPTER ELEVEN

Thoughts of Leticia consumed Oliver's dreams, he worried if she was crying, or sad because of him, and he found it hard to focus. To think that at one time, he never imagined himself falling for someone else!

After Freya had left him and subsequently died, Oliver shut the doors of his heart completely to love. That was until Leticia came along and snuck in through the cracks. He hadn't realized how much he cared for her until he lost her.

Oliver paused when he arrived at the open ground near the creek and placed both hands behind him. It gave him a moment to steady his thoughts, he had to get this right.

In front of him, Leticia was sitting in the exact same spot that they had sat. She had her knees hugged to her chest, and her head was placed on them The only sound Oliver could hear was the rustling of the leaves and the running of the water.

Pain clutched his heart; was she crying, was it because of him?

Leticia sat still. The hem of her light blue gown billowed in the breeze, and she held on to her scarf with her hand, allowing the wind to twist it in different directions.

"Leticia," Oliver called her gently, before walking over to her. "Why are you here?" The words were much starker than he wanted. They sounded like an accusation when he just wanted to say hello.

Startled, Leticia lifted her head and was visibly surprised to see him. She staggered to her feet and lowered her head as she fiddled with her fingers.

"Why'd you come?" she asked softly.

Oliver threw his hands in the air and emitted a short sigh. "I was worried, I guess. I couldn't find you anywhere, so I decided to look for you. Were you not enjoying the party?"

Leticia shrugged her shoulders. "I was. Or I am. I just came out because I needed some fresh air."

Oliver placed both hands behind him once more, trying to keep them still for he was suddenly full of nerves. "Why don't I think you actually enjoyed the party?" He offered her a slight smile but worried that his nerves might have twisted it into a grimace.

"I'm happy, Doctor Randall..."

"Don't do that, Leticia," Oliver said, taking a step forward. "Don't treat me like a stranger just because we had a disagreement."

"A disagreement?"

"Call me Oliver," he said. "Please. I'd feel more comfortable if you do."

Leticia glanced at him and turned to watch the creek. "Like I was saying, I am happy for Carolyn and Sherman. I'm happy they got married, finally. I'm happy for Maggie and Edwin. Their future is just starting and I am really excited to plan their wedding. Soon, they will become Mr. and Mrs. Grant."

Oliver smiled softly. "Is that the same thing you want for yourself? That kind of happiness?"

Leticia turned to him and crossed her arms. "Of course. Who doesn't want to be happy? I admit it. I want someone to look at me like Sherman looks at Carolyn. I want someone to look out for me like Maggie looks out for Edwin. I want a reason to smile. But I understand that not everyone is going to have a fairytale ending and that's all right. It's sad, but it's all right."

"It's not all right. You deserve to find happiness too. You deserve your own fairytale ending."

Leticia squinted her eyes at him. "No offense, Oliver, but you are in no position to talk to me. You basically put a bridge between us because you learned about my past. A past, I'll remind you, that I had no choice in."

"I wasn't trying to hurt you," Oliver tried to explain.

"Don't get me wrong. I'm not angry. I'm not angry at you for not wanting someone as damaged as I am. I can't blame you for looking out for your own interest. It was different for Carolyn and Edwin, that's why I envy them. If I had gotten over my heartbreak sooner, I might have had a shot at falling in love and meeting someone special before I arrived here in Appleton. But my heart still hadn't healed. Sherman loved Carolyn from the first day he laid eyes on her. Edwin too. It didn't take them many meetings for their feelings to show. They have a history. My past? Our past?

They lived it together. Sherman and Edwin saved us from an awful situation and they went through the struggle together with their partners. They know what it was like, and they know who we are despite that past. That's why I cannot blame you. You're an outsider, Oliver. You weren't there, so how can I expect you to understand? It's only natural that you want to keep your distance from me."

Oliver sighed. "Leticia, I did not mean to hurt you with my actions."

"It's not what you did, it's what you didn't do," Leticia said. "If you truly liked me – if your feelings were so strong and supposedly true, then why didn't you come to me at the dinner? Why did you stay away? Why did you turn away from me? I'm not a child, Oliver. I saw you. I saw the look in your eyes."

Oliver took a step back and ran his fingers through his hair. He was dumbfounded. Again, Leticia was right. If he liked her that much, why did her past matter to him? Why was he overreacting?

Leticia slowly nodded. "I see you have nothing to say. It's not surprising. I didn't actually expect you to justify your actions. Please, excuse me, I should be with my friends right now."

She turned to leave and slowly began to walk out of the field. Oliver stood there and watched her, feeling a pain in his heart. There was no way he was letting her leave like that. Not again.

"Letty..."

Oliver rushed after her, reached for her hand, and took it. Leticia paused in her tracks but she didn't turn back around. Before Oliver could plead his case, he heard hurried footsteps approaching. They were fast. Really fast. Before he could turn to see what was approaching them with such haste, he felt a sharp, painful blow to the back of his head. He had been hit by something! The world spun and he slowly fell to the ground, his fingers slipping from Leticia's wrist.

The last thing he saw was Leticia's horrified face as she stared at the figure standing over him with a gun in his hand. The man had an evil smirk on his face.

"Well, if it isn't my lucky day. Who would have thought I'd run into you, Leticia!"

Oliver could barely hear. Just as Leticia made to scream, another man appeared on the scene and placed a firm hand over Leticia's mouth. Leticia's struggle was the last thing Oliver saw before everything went completely dark.

CHAPTER TWELVE

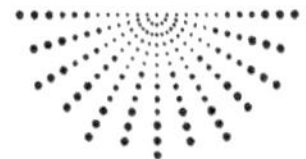

*L*eticia's eyelids were heavy. Too heavy. She had been struggling to open them for a minute but to no avail. All she could do was blink slowly, each blink sent a knife of pain through her skull but it was easing off.

Where was she?

The more she blinked, the more she could see and the pain was now bearable. After about ten minutes, she could keep her eyes open.

Fear stroked an ice-cold hand down her spine as she became aware of her surroundings. She squinted her eyes and scanned the room, someone was panting. She tried to understand what was going on and where she was and realized it was her. She was almost hyperventilating with fear, likely to go into a faint. Leticia didn't faint, that was for weaker ladies than she was.

Taking a breath she slowed her breathing and realized her hands were bound behind her back and her legs were bound together at her ankles.

It seemed like they were in a cottage. A dark and burnt cottage, given the black charred wood walls and overbearing smell of ash. It looked familiar but she was too confused to think. The sun was already setting, seen through some dusty and charred curtain and the room was dim.

Leticia's head hurt badly, and the sound of her palpitating heart wasn't helping her concentrate. She needed to think, to find a way out of this.

Closing her eyes to steady her breathing she tried to remember what had happened. She backtracked, trying to figure out what in the world she was doing here. How did she get here? Her memory was still so foggy, and the pain in the side of her head was beginning to throb once more.

"Porter..."

Then it clicked. Leticia gasped, recalling Porter Hathaway's face just before she had blacked out. It didn't seem real, and she would have convinced herself that she imagined it if she wasn't tied up in a burnt-out cottage. Leticia felt her blood chill. No one knew she was there, and if Porter truly kidnapped her, then she was in danger. A lot of danger.

"Oh, why did I leave the party?" she groaned, on the verge of tears.

This was no good, she must remain in control. If she let her fear rule then she was lost. Scanning the room, her breath caught in her throat when she saw a figure slumped in the deeper shadows in the corner. She froze, startled by the strange figure.

Keeping very still she peered at it, trying to figure out if it was a threat to her or not. Mixed feelings of relief and fear washed over her when she realized it was Oliver in an unconscious state.

"Oh, my goodness. Oliver!" Leticia gasped and scooted over to his side. "Oliver, are you all right?"

Leticia groaned and continued to move over to his side, little by little until she reached him. "Oliver? Doctor Randall?"

He wasn't responding. Oliver was still. Pain engulfed her but she forced it down and listened, she could just hear him breathing. Leticia nudged him on the shoulders repeatedly but he didn't move on his own.

What should she do? Another shiver ran through her but this one was because it was cold. Reaching out, she felt Oliver, he was cold too. She drew in a shaky breath and moved even closer to Oliver as tears welled up in her eyes. Maybe they could keep each other warm.

"Oliver?"

Why was he so still? Why wasn't he responding? Leticia nudged him again as she began to fear the worst. She recalled seeing him crash to the ground after Porter had hit him with the butt of his gun. Oliver had not only fallen to the ground, but he had hit his head again. What if the fall had done something to him? What if...

"Oh, dear Lord, help us," Leticia's voice quaked and she closed her eyes to pray. Feeling more grounded knowing that the Lord would send aid if He could she opened her eyes. "Oliver! Wake up, please."

As if he heard her call, or felt her fear, Oliver drew in a very deep breath and coughed. He groaned loudly and lifted his head as he searched the room frantically. He was in a daze, and his breathing became labored.

Oliver muttered incoherent words and struggled with the ropes. All the while, Leticia sat quietly leaning against him, offering what comfort she could, waiting for him to gather himself.

"Oliver, it's me," she whispered.

Oliver turned to her and a sigh of relief slipped from his lips. "I'm sorry, I was a bit confused. Why are we here?"

"You know this place?" Leticia asked. "Where are we?"

"We're at my cottage, at the end of my property," Oliver revealed. "It got burnt pretty badly during the time Edwin stayed here. I haven't had the time to rebuild it."

"Oh, the cottage," Leticia said, recalling why it looked so familiar. That was a relief, it was behind the doctor's house and clinic, they had not been whisked away in the night. Of course, it was empty and no one would come here looking for them. "Are you all right, Oliver? It took you a while to wake up. Does it hurt anywhere?"

"I should be asking you," Oliver said and groaned. "Are you all right, Letty? What happened? Did they drag you here? Did they hurt you?"

"To be honest, I have no idea what happened myself," Leticia admitted. "I woke up and the last thing I remember was being muffled by a large hand over my mouth. My head hurts, and I am so confused and scared."

"It's all right to be scared, Letty," Oliver told her. "We'll get out of this, I promise you. I won't let anything happen to you."

Leticia's lips began to quiver. "Oh, Oliver, I'm so sorry. This was exactly what I was trying to explain. This was the reason I said I understood why you didn't want to be with me. If we had never met, you would not be in this predicament right now. It's all my fault, and I am so sorry. This was exactly what we were running from. This vile man. Now, you're trapped in this."

Oliver smiled weakly and leaned on the wall. "Letty, no. For once, listen to me. This isn't on you. It's on me. I should have done a better job of protecting you and keeping you safe. This... this is all my fault. If I had just said yes when Edwin asked me to dance with you, then you wouldn't have left the party. You wouldn't have left your friends. But I was scared you didn't want me to dance with you because I hurt you, so I declined. This is on me. Now look, you are at the mercy of the men that ruined your life."

Leticia could see the sincerity in his eyes. It melted her heart, and she was sure he was being truthful. Oliver blamed himself.

"It's not your fault, and it's not mine either then." Leticia smiled. "Let's just blame the villains in my life that refuse to leave us alone."

"Are you sure you're all right?" Oliver asked, assessing her. "You're not hurt anywhere? No bruises, nothing?"

Leticia slowly shook her head. "Knowing who Porter is, I can guess his objective here. If he didn't come to kill us, he came to take us back. And if it's the latter, then he won't physically hurt me since I'd be useful to him. I just don't understand how he found us. We were very discreet in our travels, and we came all the way to South Dakota. How exactly did he trail us?"

"I'm sure men like him have their ways," Oliver said. "If he came here seeking revenge against you and your friends for running away from him, then I'm guessing he's really angry. If he is, who knows what he plans on doing with you three?"

Leticia sighed. "Why now?" she whispered. "Things were only starting to look up for us. Haven't we suffered enough?"

"Letty, there was another man," Oliver said. "The one that gagged you. Do you have any idea who he is?"

"I do," she nodded. "Brandon Eckert. I really hate that man."

"He's the one that forced Carolyn into a fake marriage with him, isn't he?" Oliver asked.

Leticia nodded. "He not only forced her into a fake marriage, but he also tried to force himself on her. Sherman stepped in just in time to save her. To save us all. That man is as evil as they come."

"It's truly odd how they were desperate enough to follow you all down here," Oliver said. "I'll find a way out of this, Leticia, I promise you. Trust me."

"I trust you," she said without hesitation. "And I feel safe having you close to me. Honestly, I would probably be losing my mind if I was here all alone. I'm sorry I dragged you into this, but I'm happy you're here."

Oliver smiled and began to writhe against the ropes. He stifled his groans, as he tried to find a way out.

Leticia did the same with her hands and feet. She strained so hard, but the ropes were tied on too tightly and all she was achieving was to have them cut into her skin.

"It's hopeless," Leticia said, nearly out of breath. "The ropes are knotted too tightly. I can't pull my hand out."

"We can try. Those men don't seem to be around at the moment, so now is our chance to find a way out of here. We can only try."

Leticia didn't want to admit it, but she was exhausted. She was too tired to do anything. She had barely eaten and her throat was incredibly dry. She wondered how long they had been there at the cottage. She wondered if they ruined the party with their disappearance, or if everyone was out looking for them. Leticia didn't want to think of how worried Carolyn and Margaret were going to be when they realized that she was gone. It hurt her heart to imagine that Porter had gone after them too at the wedding.

"No, Sherman and Edwin are there to protect them," she whispered.

It was the second time Porter Hathaway had held her hostage. Perhaps, that was her sign to stop going for walks. Leticia wondered what Porter's plan was with her. What was it that he wanted?

As if on cue, the door was flung wide open. Leticia gasped loudly as she watched Porter and Brandon strut into the room with their guns drawn. Fear curled like a snake in her gut, but like a snake, her anger rose and was quick and ready to strike.

Porter walked up to Leticia slowly and squatted in front of her. His face still scared her, and his gaze was cold. Leticia tried so hard not to show emotions but her chest was rising and falling fast.

"Oh, Leticia," Porter finally said. "Did you miss me?"

"What do you want, Porter? Why can't you just leave us alone?"

Porter turned to Brandon and they both chuckled. "Leave you alone? Oh, no. That won't do. I am going to get all my girls back in line, one by one, and then restore my business to its former glory..."

Porter traced the cold barrel of his gun across her cheek.

"...Starting with you, Leticia."

CHAPTER THIRTEEN

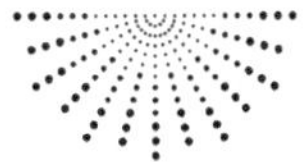

"You seem troubled, Maggie," Edwin said, placing his hand on Margaret's.

Margaret touched the back of his hand and squeezed it gently. Sometimes, she wondered how Edwin was so quick to pick up on things. He could always tell when she was in a good mood, or when she was deep in thought. Sometimes, all it took was for him to hold her hand and he could easily guess that something was bothering her. Margaret had no idea how he was able to do this, but she was thankful for the skill. She didn't have to tell Edwin when something was on her mind, he always knew when she wanted to talk.

"I'm not troubled. I was just thinking, that's all," Margaret said.

"What were you thinking about?"

"This ceremony," Margaret said with a sigh. "It is so beautiful. Sherman and Carolyn look to be in their own world. I just really love the fact that they got their happy ending. It's like a ray of hope for Leticia and me. Carolyn had never fallen in love before. She was orphaned at a young age and was alone all her life. Well, at least until she met us. Now, look at her, happily married, to a good man who loves her with all his heart. I'm happy for her, and just thinking about our wedding makes my stomach tingle."

Edwin leaned in and took Margaret's hand into his. He planted a kiss on it and caressed the back of her palm. "I'm happy that I met you, my love. I promise you – I may be lacking in sight, but I promise that I will try to make you happy, Maggie. Our union will be wonderful, I believe it to be so."

"I do too," Margaret answered.

"I never really wanted to do anything, you know?" Edwin continued. "My plan before was to just get something to do with my hands. Sherman had agreed to help me with work. I was all right taking on easy work because all I wanted, all I was content with, was you. But Samantha brought up the idea of braille, and now, I want more. I don't just want to settle for less. I want to give you the best, Maggie. Because you deserve the best. When I finish learning braille, I will make sure I get a job, teaching children at that school for the blind. I'll do it."

Margaret placed her hand on his cheek. "I know you will. You've made so much progress with braille. I have no doubt this is just the beginning of a wonderful future with you. Edwin, I am excited."

"Me too." Edwin chuckled. "But I need to point something out first, Maggie. I cannot live without you. And no, I'm not saying it because I don't have my sight anymore, or because I need you to help me move around, I'm saying it because it's true. I had already given up on life. I was done. This... blindness took its toll on me. At one point, it defeated me. I wondered what use I was to the world without my sight. But then, you came along. You came to me at that cottage and saved me from myself. I live for you now, and strangely, I am much happier at this very moment, than I was when we first got here."

Margaret reached her hands over his neck and hugged him. "I am too," she whispered into his ear.

Her eyes bounced off different people at the party, all giggling and chatting loudly. Margaret's eyebrows furrowed. She slowly let go of Edwin and continued to scan the party.

"Where's Leticia?" she whispered, rising to her feet. "I haven't seen her in several hours. It's getting late."

"She's probably in the kitchen," Edwin answered.

Margaret shook her head. "No, I just came back from the kitchen, she isn't there. Maybe she went for a walk to clear her head."

"Yes, maybe. She should be back soon."

"Yes, but it's been hours," she whispered again and brought her hands to her hips. "There's no way she would miss the entire party. She hasn't danced yet or had her dessert, and Letty likes her desserts."

"Oh, that one is particularly true," Edwin said, standing up too. "Do you want to go look for her? Maybe she lost track of time."

"Maybe," Margaret said. "I'll go. Are you going to be all right by yourself? I won't be long."

Edwin chuckled. "I'll survive."

Margaret leaned forward and placed a peck on his cheek. "Good, give me a minute."

With that Margaret picked up her jacket and made her way out of the party. She stood outside the church and looked to her right, then her left. There was no way Leticia went back to the restaurant. She loved walks, so instead, Margaret figured she would go somewhere quiet. If that was the case, then she would walk towards the outskirts of the town, in the direction of the doctor's house.

"Excuse me?" Margaret said, grabbing the attention of a lady standing by the fence. "Have you seen Leticia by any chance?"

"The doctor went looking for her about two hours ago," another man answered in the lady's stead. "He went that way. That's the same path Leticia took."

"Thank you," Margaret said with a smile.

Her guess had been correct. Margaret began to walk down the path, in search of Leticia. It was evening, and soon, the sun was going to set. Margaret and Leticia still had a lot to do at the church before they had to go back to the restaurant. They had to clean up, do the dishes, and make sure the church was spotless. The sooner they started, the better, but it wasn't this thought that drove her, she was starting to worry.

Margaret reached the creek and brought both hands to her mouth. "Letty!" she yelled, panting. "Where are you?"

The next stop had to be the doctor's house. It was not far from there, and from what Margaret had heard, Oliver owned the property from the creek, all the way to the local clinic. Perhaps, Leticia went to see Oliver.

Just as she was about to make her way to the clinic, a gust of wind blew, causing her to raise her arms so they protected her eyes. When the gust stopped and she dropped her gaze, her eyes picked up on a scarf tumbling on the ground. At first, she didn't think much of it, but then she froze in her steps when it clicked. Margaret tried to pick it up but it was still a little windy so she had to chase it about as the breeze pulled it in different directions. Once she was able to get a grip on it, she gazed down, her brow furrowed with worry.

"This is Leticia's..." she mumbled. "What is it doing here... and where's Leticia?"

Margaret scanned the field underneath the white elm trees. She turned, trying to search for anything else that belonged to Leticia. But instead, she saw a leaf, stained with blood. Then, she saw another, all with droplets of blood on them.

"Oh, my."

Without sparing a moment to think, Margaret ran as fast as her legs could take her, back to the church. One thing she had learned over the years was to trust her gut feeling because it was never wrong. And in that moment, her gut feeling was awful. It felt like the reign of terror had begun, and it had gotten to Leticia first.

"Carolyn! Sherman!" Margaret yelled at them, holding Leticia's scarf up.

They must have sensed the fear in her voice. Carolyn and Sherman exchanged glances and walked over to meet Margaret where she had stopped beside Edwin. Margaret held on to Edwin's hand, trying to catch her breath.

"What is it, Margaret?" Edwin asked. "What's wrong? What happened?"

"Maggie, what happened to you?" Carolyn asked. "You look like you've seen a ghost."

"I think Leticia is in danger. I found her scarf by the creek, and there was blood too, and she's nowhere to be seen. They are here, Carolyn. They've come for us."

Sherman stepped forward and took the scarf from Margaret's hand. "There's blood on this too," he said, turning it over in his hands.

Carolyn covered her mouth with her palms. "Oh, Lord. Oh, Lord, please help us."

"Wait, what did you say, Maggie?" Sam was by their side, concern etched on her face. "My father went to look for Leticia. I've been waiting for him but he isn't back yet."

"I think they both got into trouble," Margaret said. "I didn't see either of them, and I was sure they would be together."

"Why?" Edwin asked. "Why did Doctor Randall go after Leticia?"

"They have been courting for a while," Carolyn said. "We don't know what happened in the past few days, but Maggie and I think they had a disagreement. Leticia has no idea that we know about it, as we were waiting for her to open up to us. If this is Porter Hathaway, then he has Doctor Randall too."

"I'll get a few of the parishioners, some horses, and a wagon and we'll be on our way," Sherman said. "Edwin, I'll leave the ladies here with you."

"I'm coming too," Samantha said. "I'm going to help find them. Leticia wouldn't have left the party if it wasn't for my father. I want to help and you might need a doctor."

"Me too," Margaret said. "We're coming along."

"It might be dangerous, I don't think that's a good idea," Sherman said.

"Please, don't stop us," Samantha stared him down, her face determined. "You need all the help you can get. I'm not staying here."

Sherman turned to Carolyn who gave him a subtle nod. "All right, you both can come along. Carolyn, please stay here with Edwin and send everyone else home. We'll take some horses, and we'll be back soon."

Carolyn nodded. She raised up on her tiptoes and placed a kiss on Sherman's cheek. "Be safe."

"I will." He squeezed her hands and stared into her eyes for long moments before turning to leave.

Edwin turned to Margaret and gave her a hug. "I know I can't force you to stay back, but please be careful,

Maggie. Don't put yourself in any danger and come back to me. I wish I could do more to help, but I can't."

Margaret stroked his back. "It's all right, Edwin. I'll be back soon, I promise."

"Let's go," Sherman said.

Margaret was on the verge of tears. She was terrified at the thought that Porter Hathaway had returned. This time, he was going to ruin their lives for sure. If he could travel all the way from Minnesota just for their sake, then the man didn't come to play games. He came for revenge.

The mere thought of it scared Margaret to her very core.

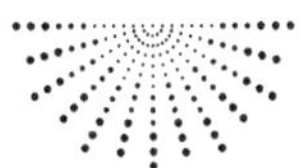

CHAPTER FOURTEEN

Leticia watched Oliver slowly open his eyes. She had sobbed all through the beating he'd received. Now he had purple bruises on his face and arms and she was sure elsewhere. Porter had taken his time, kicking Oliver in the gut and taking out all his anger on him. Then, he proceeded to hit Leticia too and ripped at her gown. The tough material tore a little but thankfully held. All the while, Brandon sat in the corner and watched, drinking from a bottle of whiskey that occasionally shook in his hands.

"I think I heard something outside," Porter said to Brandon. "I'll go check."

"Aren't you worried that the owner of this cottage will be back soon?" Brandon asked. "We've been here a while."

"No one's coming here," Porter said. "Can't you see it's abandoned, you fool?"

"I was just asking," Brandon stuttered. "I mean, it's better to be safe than sorry, isn't it? I don't want any surprises."

"If anyone comes here, I'll handle them. That's why we have guns." Porter shook his head, as if in exasperation. "Now stop acting like a wimp, and watch them closely. I'll be back once I check the area and make sure we're alone."

"All right. Fine."

Porter turned back to Leticia with a smirk on his face. "When I return, Leticia, I'll have to teach you some manners. We'll have some fun too. I haven't had any fun in a long time and you can guess whose fault that is. But first, I'll have to find Carolyn since she was the mastermind behind the entire escape. Also, I'd love to see her reunited with her husband. Don't you think that will be sweet?"

Leticia glared at him without saying a word. She turned her attention back to Oliver when Porter had left the room. Oliver was bleeding from his head. He had taken some hard punches to the chin and it looked swollen now. He also had a black eye. Leticia felt her blood boil, just seeing Oliver suffer like that for something that didn't concern him.

She wished Porter was dead, Brandon too. Leticia had killed them so many times in her head, that it didn't seem like a horrible idea to enact the plan in real life. These men were the worst people on the Earth. It was hard to tell how their minds worked. How could people be this evil? And for what? What right did they have?

"Leticia?" Oliver called out to her weakly.

"Oliver!" Leticia said, feeling a rush of energy course through her body. She was about to move to his side, but Oliver moved towards her first. He groaned and sat by her side, their hands still tied behind their backs.

"Are you all right?" he asked, assessing her. "Your lip is bleeding."

Leticia's lips curved downward at the sides. "I should be asking if you are all right. You received quite a beating because of me and you're bleeding everywhere. I'm so sorry, Oliver. This is all my fault."

Oliver shook his head. "How long was I unconscious?"

"Only a few minutes," Leticia answered. "He stopped when you passed out and started hitting me instead. I was wrong. He's here for revenge, and he doesn't care if I look beaten and bruised. He's going to drag us back to Minnesota in whatever state we're in. In fact, I think he wants us to look beaten so when he gets back home, he can brag to his friends that he got the three of us back in line."

"Are you sure you're all right, Leticia? What did he do to you?" Oliver asked. "Why's your gown all torn?"

Leticia looked down at the gown and sighed. Porter had managed to rip the lower half of her gown, and the sleeves too. Leticia knew his plan was to force himself on her, but she had given him a hard time even with her hands tied behind her back.

"He didn't do anything," she said. "It'll take a lot more that ripping my clothes to shake me. Don't you worry."

"I'm sorry, Letty. There isn't much I can do to help you right now," Oliver said.

"There's nothing to apologize for," Leticia said. "We'll get out of this, I have to believe so."

Oliver nodded. "And you're not going back to Minnesota. Never. I will do everything in my power to stop that from happening. Don't worry about how bruised I look. We'll get out of this even if it's the last thing I do."

Leticia glanced at Brandon who was having a moment with his bottle of whiskey and leaned into Oliver. "They have no idea that this is your cottage, Oliver."

Oliver raised his eyebrows. "What? Really?"

Leticia nodded. "Before Porter left, Brandon shared his worry that the owners of the cottage might come and find us here. They don't know."

"My house, the clinic is just in front of us," Oliver said. "I'm worried that Samantha might come home and they'll see her from here."

Leticia slumped her shoulders. "That's true. Your house really isn't that far from here. What if she decided to come here to the cottage? That won't be good. These men are dangerous, I don't want them to see Sam. Who knows the ideas they'll get seeing her all by herself?"

"I know," Oliver said with a sigh. "That's why we need to get out of here by ourselves. I have a feeling that our friends will realize we aren't there. Someone might be looking for us already."

"I doubt it," Leticia said. "Now that I think about it, I regret not telling Carolyn and Margaret about our relationship. I didn't want to tell them too soon. They don't know we're together, Oliver. Or that we were courting."

Oliver squinted his eyes. "I think they do."

Leticia shook her head. "No, they don't. I haven't told them."

"I'm pretty sure they do, Letty," Oliver insisted.

"Why do you think so?"

"That day when I picked you up and took you to the creek, they saw us. You were getting into the wagon, and they were standing by the window, peeking out at us. I saw them and I waved, and they waved back. They know, Leticia."

Leticia's jaw dropped. It was all starting to make sense. Now she understood why they never questioned her when she insisted on going to town, wearing new shoes, when she constantly combed her hair to make sure it was tidy... they always asked if she was all right, but they didn't say anything. They were waiting for her to come to them. They were waiting for Leticia to be confident enough to tell them about her relationship.

"Oh, for Pete's sake," Brandon groaned. "When did I finish this?"

Brandon dropped the bottle to the ground and rubbed his hands roughly all over his face. His skin was red, and his eyes were barely open. Leticia noticed that he looked worse than he had back in Minnesota. His belly was more protruding, and he looked miserable. If she had to guess, it was either he didn't want to be there, or he had lost the stomach for revenge.

"Listen, Leticia," Oliver said. "He is drunk, and I think we can make our way past him. If we can free ourselves."

Leticia nodded. "I think so too."

"Now, I found a nail back there. I was working on getting my ropes lose, but I'm too weak to continue. Here, take the nail. Turn around and sit facing Brandon, but with your back towards me. We can help each other."

Leticia obeyed. She turned her back to Oliver and they leaned on each other. Oliver handed her the nail, and she began to pick at the rope as much as she could. Oliver helped her pull the ropes apart as she worked with the nail tirelessly, despite it cramping her fingers and rubbing her wrists raw. Finally, they heard a snap.

Leticia gasped. "It's loose," she whispered. "My hands are free."

"Good, now undo the ropes around your feet," Oliver whispered. "Hurry, his eyes are closed."

"Wait, let me free your hands first," Leticia insisted.

"No, it's better if one of us is free," Oliver said. "Undo the ropes first, and then you can undo mine. Come on, Leticia, there's no time."

Leticia kept her eyes fixed on Brandon as she quickly untied her feet. Her palms were sweaty, and the sound of her heartbeat was so loud, that it terrified her. Soon, her legs were free, and she rose to her feet without hesitation. She reached for Oliver's feet and began to undo the ropes.

"Hurry, Letty," he whispered.

"What do you think you're doing?" Brandon roared and rose to his feet. He staggered a little, unable to find his footing.

"Hurry, Letty."

"I'm trying."

As she tried to undo the last knot, Brandon grabbed her ankle and yanked her hand. Leticia screamed. Kicking out, she tried to pry her foot from his grip but he didn't let go. He pulled her, dragging her closer and closer to him.

"Oliver!" Leticia kicked and screamed.

Brandon climbed on top of her with the rope and tried to force her arms together. Leticia fought, trying to get him off her body. The more she fought, the weaker she got. Just as she was about to lose all strength, Oliver dived at Brandon, slamming into his belly with a head-butt. He had managed to get the last knot on his legs free, but his hands were still tied behind his back.

"Run, Leticia," Oliver ordered, forcing Brandon to the ground with his shoulders.

Leticia froze on the spot, shaking. "I can't."

Disorientated, Brandon groaned on the ground and his eyes were closing. Oliver left his side and moved to Leticia.

"There's no time, go. Now. Go get some help. Porter will return soon, and given all the ruckus, he might already be on his way back."

Leticia shook her head and reached for Oliver's ropes. "No."

"Letty, he has a gun."

"I'm not leaving you, Oliver. I know Porter, and I know how dangerous that man is. If I leave you here, he will hurt you so badly before I even return with any help. He will wreak unbelievable cruelty if he is given the chance to return and find you here."

"Letty..."

"Just give me some time," Leticia said. "The ropes are tight, that's why. Do you want to know why Porter is really angry? It's not just about us running away, Oliver. It's not. It's not just about us refusing to do his bidding. We ruined his business. We freed all of the girls working at the saloon. That's why he's angry. If I run away, and leave you here, he'll kill you in anger. I'm not letting that happen.

Oliver lowered his head and nodded. "All right. I just pray that we both get away before he returns."

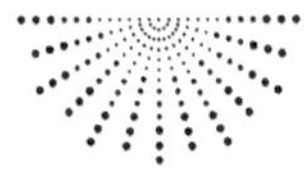

CHAPTER FIFTEEN

"The more I think about it, the more certain I am," Samantha said. "We own this property, so I think they should be here somewhere."

Margaret picked at her fingers as she nervously scanned the path. They had asked a total of seven people if they had seen any unfamiliar faces in the town that evening, and they had said no. They had run into Mrs. Doris, the owner of the only inn in the town, and she too had claimed that no one fit Porter's description at the inn.

"They couldn't have skipped town," Sherman said. "Knowing Porter, he is probably going to try his luck and get all three of you. They have to be somewhere."

But where? ... Margaret shut her eyes to think. There was blood, which meant that Leticia and Oliver were probably unconscious when they were carted away by Porter. But they were two grown people. There was no way he could have gone far when he had to drag Leticia and Oliver with him.

"The cottage," Margaret said. "It's not far from here, and everyone knows it burned down. If Porter took Leticia, then he probably took her when she was unconscious because Letty wouldn't go without a fight. Oliver is a big man. So, I'm also thinking he has help."

"Brandon Eckert," Sherman rasped.

"I think we should check the cottage first to be sure," Samantha said. "Maggie is right. It's the closest place to the creek that they could have taken them. It's also a place no one goes anymore, so no one will look there first."

Sherman paused to think. "All right, let's check out the cottage first."

The horses galloped down in a steady motion. The familiar feeling of guilt that had made living miserable for Margaret back in Minnesota was slowly creeping up to her. Margaret was worried sick. She really believed that they had left the past behind them. What she failed to take into account, was the fact that Porter was a disturbed man with the tendency of becoming obsessive.

"It's all right. We'll find them," Samantha told her. "You look like you'll pass out at any second."

Margaret turned to her. "It's my fault. A part of me wishes that I had never urged Carolyn and Leticia to come out west. It all boils down to me and my spontaneous decision. We had suffered so much during the war that I was so desperate for a change in our lives. It's all on me. If I had not picked up the newspaper that day. If I had not seen that advert. We'll still be back in New Hampshire, living slightly less miserable lives."

"I heard about your story, Maggie. I'm so sorry that you three had to endure all of that. While I do agree that matters did not work out the way exactly that you hoped, good things still happened. You all managed to find loving partners, Leticia included. That's happiness too. I know you would have preferred that things worked out as you had planned it, but if it did, I wouldn't have met you three. I won't have made friends, and my father would not have found love. This is only a slight hiccup in your way. You'll get through it."

"Thank you, Sam. That was comforting."

"I want to help, Maggie. I want to help put the nightmare to bed so that you, Carolyn, and Leticia can get on with the next chapter of your lives. No one deserves what you had to endure. Not when you dedicated three years of your life working during the war, saving lives."

"That was the reason for the move in the first place," Margaret explained. "It was supposed to be like a big break. After my aunt died, it felt like my life had no meaning again. I hated that feeling and I wanted it to go away. It just hurts that, things didn't go as planned. I'm thankful for Appleton and I would really want things to work out for us here. I mean, Carolyn just got married."

"Don't worry about anything," Sam told her. "You three aren't going anywhere. As I said, it's just a small hurdle you have to cross, once and for all."

"We should walk from here," Sherman suggested. "We need to be as quiet as possible. If they hear us, they could react aggressively and we don't want that."

Margaret and Sam obliged and followed Sherman's lead. They walked closely behind him, making sure their steps were as quiet as possible. Margaret had her heart in her throat as they slowly approached the cottage. She hoped and prayed that Leticia was in there, and they had not wasted time for nothing.

Of the three of them, Margaret would have preferred that Porter took her. Carolyn had hurt Brandon's pride, and Porter held her responsible for the escape since she tried to use her marriage to Brandon as a front. Leticia had tried to kill them, both Porter and Brandon. She had almost shot them with their guns. If there was anyone Porter hated the most, it had to be Leticia. It worried Margaret that he managed to take her first, of the three of them.

The sound of a thump and a continued struggle caused Margaret to gasp. She imagined Porter choking Leticia, trying to suck the life out of her.

"Leticia!" Margaret yelled and dashed towards the cottage without hesitation.

As if she heard Margaret's cry, Leticia groaned loudly, further convincing Margaret that something was happening to her. Once she reached the door, Margaret pushed it open and staggered into the room. Her eyes fell on Oliver first who was bruised all over.

"Dad!" Sam yelled, rushing to his side. "Dad, are you all right? What happened to you?"

Sherman stormed into the room too, his hands curled into a fist. He was visibly angry and ready to take on someone. But Margaret had frozen in fear, scared that something had happened to Leticia. She had stopped groaning immediately after Margaret entered the room.

"Leticia," Oliver called out to her.

Margaret followed his gaze to the corner of the room. She gasped at the sight she beheld. It wasn't Porter on the floor, it was Brandon. Leticia sat on him and had her hand on his neck. She lifted her right hand up in the air and formed a fist with it. Then she brought it down, landing a clean blow on his face.

"Leticia!" Margaret said breathlessly.

"Don't you ever!" Leticia yelled. "Don't you ever come after the people I care about again. Enough! You do not own us."

Margaret rushed to Leticia's side and pulled her off the man. She gathered her in her arms, not letting her go. Sherman quickly found a rope and he tied Brandon's hands and feet together.

"Are you all right, Dad?" Sam asked Oliver. "Can you keep your eyes open?"

Oliver nodded. "I can. I'm all right. It's just a few bruises."

Margaret cupped Leticia's face with her hands and studied it. "Take a deep breath," she asked. "You need to calm down."

"He tried to kill Oliver, Maggie," Leticia said, out of breath. "Porter too. He beat us, ripped my clothes, and said vile things. All of this, for what? What did we do to deserve this sort of treatment from these men?"

"It's my fault," Margaret whispered. "Blame me. I deserve to be punished for this. I thought we were past it. I thought we were far from all of this, but it is now clear that Porter Hathaway will not leave us alone."

"I deserve to be punished, Maggie," Leticia said. "Look at Oliver. He is like this because of me. I watched him get beaten to a pulp by Porter for something he knows nothing about."

"It's over now," Margaret told her. "We'll find a way out of this, we have to. I don't plan on leaving this town. We're not leaving, and to do that, we have to fight to stay. We'll fight this."

Leticia nodded. "Where's Carolyn?"

"She's with Edwin back at the church."

"How did you even find us?" Leticia asked, sitting up.

"I went out looking for you and Oliver, and when I got to the creek, I saw the scarf with blood on it. That was when I realized you were in trouble. It's a new dress you bought for the wedding. There's no way you would have dropped the scarf. We figured that the cottage was the closest place they could drag you to. So, we came here to check it first. Thankfully, we found you both."

"I'm going to take my dad to the clinic," Sam said, helping Oliver to his feet. "I need to clean his bruises."

"All right." Sherman nodded. "We'll be with you once we figure this out. Lock the doors to the clinic once you get in. This is just one person. The real culprit is still out there."

"I will."

Margaret watched Sam leave with Oliver who could barely walk. She turned to Leticia and watched her fiddle with her fingers.

"Aren't you going to go with him? You also need to check your bruises too."

"Later," Leticia answered.

"You all think Porter is going to go down this easily?" Brandon's voice startled them all. "You think you can defeat him?"

"Brandon, I will advise you to stay quiet," Sherman said to him. "I am trying so hard to keep myself from hitting you."

Brandon sniggered. "Porter will not go down quietly. Do you think he doesn't have a plan? You think we didn't come here with a plan?! We knew about the wedding. We heard all about your great achievements in the paper, Preacher. If you were trying to hide, then you should have done a better job. We didn't come here to play. We came for revenge, and we're not leaving until we get it. We knew this was going to happen, we knew you'd come for that one. Leaving the real prize..."

Margaret gasped and turned to Sherman. "Carolyn."

CHAPTER SIXTEEN

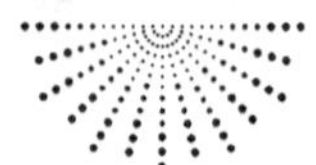

Carolyn paced back and forth. She was incapable of calming down. Her thoughts were all over the place, and she had given up on trying to slow her rapidly beating heart down. She had dreaded this day for the longest time. All the sleepless nights she had suffered, worrying about her past, were not all in vain. Carolyn had every reason to be worried. She was living her worst nightmare.

It had to happen on her wedding day, of all days. Porter returned to her life on her happiest day. It had taken Carolyn a long time to convince herself that he was never going to find them. It took her weeks to convince herself that it was all in the past. They expected Porter to be occupied, trying to restore his saloon to its former glory, not to trail them across the country for revenge. Carolyn didn't know what to make of it.

There could be many reasons why Porter was back. To kill them, to take them back? To ruin their reputation? Carolyn's head hurt the more she thought about it. If he came to kill them, then she feared he might have hurt Leticia horribly, but if he came to take them back, then he needed Leticia in good condition. But for his reputation... he would hurt them to give an example to others. Carolyn shuddered just thinking about it and prayed that her friend would be safe.

Sherman had more to lose. Carolyn groaned and lifted her head to the ceiling. She had feared that the day would come when her past would come back to haunt her future. If people found out that she worked in a saloon in Minnesota, they were going to read meaning into it, thereby giving Sherman a bad name. A name Sherman had worked so hard to build. Carolyn felt the tears well up in her eyes, just thinking about it. She hated misunderstandings.

"Carolyn, sit," Edwin told her. "I'm sure they will be fine. They have to be."

Carolyn paused her pacing and stared at Edwin. He was doing a better job controlling his emotions than she was.

Carolyn knew he was more afraid than she was. He had lost his sight, and it would be difficult to defend himself if there was a need. But still, Edwin managed to remain calm.

Carolyn walked over to him and sat by his side. "They will be fine," she said to reassure him. "Soon, they will return with Leticia and Oliver. You have nothing to worry about."

"Yes," Edwin said, nodding.

The guests had all left. Carolyn scanned the hall, staring at the empty chairs and tables. To think that a while ago, there were people everywhere, dancing and partying. Just a while ago, she was the happiest woman in the world, and now, she was worrying so much, that her palms were wet with sweat.

"How did he find us?" Edwin whispered. "It must have taken weeks of travel. Why would they spend all this time, coming after you three when they had promised to stay away?"

"My explanation for that would be Porter doesn't think," Carolyn answered. "He's like a dog with a bone. He's not going to let go until he either gets what he wants or is put in his place."

Edwin sighed. "I still don't think Margaret should have gone with them. She's one of the three of you, which means that Porter is after her too. I just hope she's all right."

"Don't worry, Edwin. They are currently with Sherman. I'm sure he won't let anything happen to them," Margaret said.

Just then, Carolyn heard a wagon pull up to the church. "That must be them," she said and gasped.

She quickly sprung to her feet and hurried to the door. Her rapidly beating heart had mellowed and she could think more clearly now that Sherman had arrived. Carolyn hoped for good news. They had left less than an hour ago. That must mean that they found Leticia fast.

She opened the door and looked out, but she saw no one. She stepped out to go check when the sound of a gun cocking startled her. Porter had been right behind the door and was now standing in front of her with his gun drawn and pointed directly at her forehead. Terror coursed through her entire body. He was real. He was actually real. There, at the church.

"If it isn't Carolyn," Porter said with a smirk. "The one I have been looking for."

* * *

"Sherman, we need to hurry," Margaret said.

Margaret glanced at Brandon in the corner of the room who still strangely had a smile on his face. He was tied up now and Sam was attending to Leticia and her father. The wounds were nasty, painful, but mostly superficial, they would heal in time.

Sherman spoke to the parishioners he had sent to the woods earlier on. They had searched the woods for Porter but came back without seeing him. Sherman was giving them more orders, telling them to broaden their search around the vicinity.

Margaret couldn't get Carolyn's image out of her mind. She was with Edwin, hence they were both in danger. The tension was too much for Margaret to handle. She feared that she was going to collapse from fear at any point. What was the plan Brandon was talking about? He had refused to say any more. From the look on his face, Margaret guessed that he was confident in whatever plan they had. Was hurting Leticia also part of Porter's plan? Or was Leticia a distraction?

"Sherman!" Margaret called out to him. "We need to go."

Sherman walked up to her and nodded in agreement. "We'll soon be on our way. But I need some of the parishioners to stay back with Sam and Doctor Randall. Some of them need to stay here too and watch Brandon, while some need to go back into the woods in search of Porter. Once I'm done directing the search, we'll be on our way."

"Sherman, I don't think Porter is hiding in the woods," Margaret said. "You heard Brandon. He said they had a plan. My guess is, that Porter is in our midst. He must be on his way to the church. He might have already taken Carolyn and Edwin for all we know."

"I know. But it's better to be safe than sorry," Sherman said. "Let's go. It's just us, right?"

"Yes." Margaret nodded. "Sam and Letty are staying back to help Oliver."

"All right. We'll be on our way then."

Sherman and Margaret hurried out of the cottage and got into the wagon quickly. Just as they were about to leave, Leticia joined them.

"Leticia, should you stay back so Sam can check your injuries?" Sherman asked.

"I'm fine," she answered. "It's only a few bruises and a cut on my lip. I want to help. This is about me too."

"Don't you want to stay by Oliver's side?" Margaret asked. "He might need you. I think you should stay with him. You both need to be with each other. Sherman and I will go to the church first and check on Carolyn."

"No," Leticia protested. "I'm going. Oliver and I have an understanding."

"Letty, no." Margaret insisted. "Go to Oliver. You don't look so good."

"Maggie, I insist. I'm coming with you both. Now, can we go? There's no time to waste."

"There is no time to quarrel," Sherman said. "If Porter Hathaway is at large, and if Carolyn and Edwin need our help, we must be on our way. The sooner we get there, the better."

With that, the three of them made their way down the road, in the direction of the church. Margaret stared at Leticia inquisitively.

"What's this about?" she asked. "Why won't you stay? We know you're courting Oliver, you don't have to be secretive about it any longer."

"I'm not being secretive," Leticia argued. "It's just... I've shown my darker side to Oliver by hitting Brandon while he watched. I think it's best to leave him in the care of his daughter and the parishioners. I don't want him to see me right now and maybe... I can help end this."

Margaret knew that it wasn't the time to argue Leticia's point. Deep down, she knew the worry was valid. She had been there. Leticia had shown an unusual fury when she hit Brandon in the face. If Leticia really loved Oliver, Margaret could understand why she wouldn't want him to see her that way.

"How did Porter find you?" Sherman asked.

"I'm not sure," she replied. "He and Brandon appeared from nowhere. Oliver and I were talking to each other at the creek and all of a sudden, Porter appeared and hit him on the back of his head. Then Brandon came up from behind me and he put his hand over my mouth. I don't know what happened after that, but I completely blacked out."

"How did they know to come here to Appleton?" Margaret whispered. "They couldn't have trailed us. They aren't that smart. And they didn't follow us because we made sure."

"I think that's my fault," Sherman revealed. "I did an interview with the local newspaper and somehow, Porter and Brandon saw it. I have no idea how, but they did. That's how they were able to find us. I'm pretty sure meeting you was a coincidence. Their plan was probably to come to the wedding and disrupt things."

"But Brandon said they have a plan," Margaret chimed in. "I wonder what it is."

"He was probably fibbing," Sherman said. "Either that, or it's a stupid plan. What I know and I'm sure of is that we cannot let this go again. We need to get rid of them from our lives once and for all. That means, we cannot let them escape."

"If they do, they will just come back," Leticia said. "And if they keep coming back, we might have to move again."

"We're not moving," Margaret said sternly. "This is our home. If anyone is to leave, they should go. We don't work for him anymore. Sherman made that clear the last time we encountered them in the woods."

Margaret mellowed and drew in a deep breath to calm herself. It was unfair that they had to live in constant terror because a man tried to use them. If she, Carolyn, and Leticia were to ever live in peace without any worry in the world, then Porter and Brandon needed to disappear from their lives. It was time that they took that stand for the future. Margaret touched the ring on her finger and sighed. Appleton was her home, and she wasn't leaving.

CHAPTER SEVENTEEN

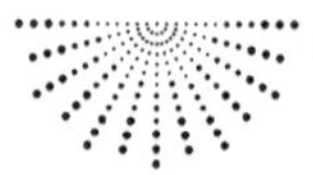

"Aren't you going to say anything to me, Carolyn? Didn't you miss me? Don't tell me you didn't look forward to my arrival."

Carolyn lifted her hands high above her head and began to step back. Several scenarios were running through her mind but at that moment, her options were limited. There was a gun pointed to her head, a large man in front of her who wanted nothing but vengeance, and no one around to help.

She was at the mercy of her worst enemy.

Porter sucked in his teeth. "If only I arrived a day earlier. I could have prevented this whole entire marriage, don't you think? How do you think Brandon is going to feel, knowing that you married someone else when you're still his wife?"

"I was never married to Brandon Eckert," Carolyn rasped.

"Does it matter? You were sold to him, so whatever he wants you to be, that you will be. We had a deal, and you broke it."

"You broke it first," Carolyn answered. "Your intentions were never to let Margaret and Leticia go. You were trying to have your cake and eat it too. What did you expect me to do?"

"Bend to my will," Porter lashed out at her hitting her hard across the cheek. It forced her backward but she kept her head high. He took a step forward, causing her to take several more back. "You were supposed to bend to my will, Carolyn. I own you. I own all of you."

"You own nothing," Carolyn spat at him. "Right from the beginning, you played us. There was never a match to be made. We heard about it from the other girls. You lie to people, promise them happiness, and then turn them into your puppets. Your slaves. And for what? Who are you?"

"Now, you want to be careful with the way you speak to me, Carolyn. I am still very much angry about my girls. Do you and your friends know what you did to me? You cost me my respect, my honor in the town. No one takes the saloon seriously anymore because my girls dared to escape! All thanks to your silly plan with that preacher."

Deep down, Carolyn was thrilled by the news. The saloon could burn to the ground for all she cared. The place was evil, and it had been her nightmare. Thinking back, Carolyn wished she had burned the place down herself. Maybe then, Porter would have been too busy building it back up to bother them.

"Porter, we let you go that day because you promised to leave us alone," Carolyn said, trying to reason with him. "Leticia didn't shoot you that day because you promised to leave us alone."

"Did you truly believe that? Did you really think I was going to leave you alone after what you did to me? Oh, you are so naïve. Do you think I was scared of the preacher? No, honey. I knew this day would come. I knew I'd get my revenge. So, here I am."

Carolyn drew in a shuddery breath.

"Get inside," he ordered. "Come on. Go."

"Porter, this is the church. You will not get away with whatever it is you're planning. People will see you, and they will come for you."

"The casualties can keep piling up then. I will kill every single person that comes my way. One at a time. Now, get inside."

Carolyn walked back into the church. She found Edwin on his feet, staring into space. He had his eyes squinted, and she could tell he was trying to listen.

"Carolyn?" Edwin said. "Is that you? Is that them?"

Porter took a step forward and peered at Edwin. "He's blind?" he said, chuckling. Porter pushed Edwin back down on the chair. "Sit back down, you pathetic wimp."

"Porter, leave him alone," Carolyn ordered.

"Carolyn, make a run for it," Edwin said, grabbing Porter's leg. "Go. I'll hold him off."

"I can't Edwin," she said. "He has a gun."

Porter pointed the gun at Edwin's head, keeping his eyes on Carolyn. "I wonder what difference it would make if I kill this one first. He's getting on my nerves, you see."

Before Carolyn could say a single word, Porter slammed the butt of the gun into Edwin's back, sending him to the floor. He continued at it, kicking and hitting Edwin with the pistol until Edwin began to cough. Carolyn made to rush to his side but Porter turned the gun back to her.

"Stay there," he roared. "This is your fault. Why are you sobbing? Shouldn't you have at least expected this?"

"You are a monster," Carolyn rasped.

"I have Leticia, and a casualty too. I have you, and this man right here, who is also a casualty. The more you resist, the more you annoy me, the more people I will kill until I'm satisfied. I'm going to start with this man right here. I'll kill him, take you, find the one with the red hair and kill anyone I find with her too."

"What do you want?" Carolyn asked, nearly in tears for Edwin.

"Revenge. Isn't it obvious? I came for my revenge and I will not leave until I'm satisfied."

Carolyn wiped her tears and dropped her hands. "Do you want to kill me? Do it, I dare you. Shoot me. You want to know something, Porter. I would rather die and be buried six feet under than return to Minnesota with you. Before you can shoot him, I'll make a run for it, and you'll be forced to shoot me because you won't catch me even if you chase me. So, I'll ask again, what is it you're here for? Spit it out."

Porter chuckled and sat down. "Well, let's see. The plan was to take you all back to Minnesota and work you like dogs until you cough out every single penny that I lost. You, Carolyn... you were supposed to be Brandon's grand prize. His reward. He would take you, and I would take the other girls. Simple."

"We're not going anywhere with you," Carolyn said.

"The second plan was to kill you all if you refused," Porter continued. "And see as how you three are not afraid of death, then that plan is going to suck. As I said, I already have Leticia and I'll take her back to Minnesota with me. The redhead, Margaret will come on her own because she has a soft spot for her friends, does she not? That's a win for me. But for Brandon? Not so much. But we can always work something out."

Carolyn figured it was better to keep him talking. The longer they spoke the more time went by. Hopefully, someone in a position to help would walk by. She stared at Edwin on the ground. He had barely moved since the beating.

"You see, I always liked you, Carolyn," Porter continued. "You are pretty, you have a nice body. Girls like you will earn me a lot of money if I invest in the right places. Now, you all managed to ruin my reputation in Minnesota, so I have two options. Take you back with me to Minnesota and repair that reputation, or take you to California and start over with you on my arm."

"What?" Carolyn felt her heart almost stop.

"What? You don't like my plan? Then perhaps, I can give you time to think while you bury your friend here," he said and pointed the gun at Edwin. "Planning his funeral will give you plenty of time to think."

"Stop. Fine," Carolyn said. "I'll go to California with you. But I'm not going back to Minnesota. And it's just going to be me. I don't want any harm coming to my friends. If I agree to break my marriage vows and work for you once again, will you leave the rest of us alone? You will leave this town, quietly?"

Porter rose to his feet, smirking. "We'll see."

Edwin groaned, pushing himself off the ground. He searched the ground with his hands for his stick. Once he had it, he sighed, trying to gather his strength.

Carolyn pitied him. It was her cross to bear, not his. He didn't deserve the beating he'd received.

"I need your word," Carolyn said. "Although you have the tendency to break it, it'll have to do. Just me, no one else."

"I said... we'll see."

With that, Porter grabbed her by the arm and dragged her with him. Her window of escape was getting smaller with each step they took, and by the time she got on that wagon with Porter, it would be difficult to escape from him.

"Don't worry, you will have plenty of ways to pay me back," Porter continued. "Since you want to do all the work for your friends, I'll let you. It'll also mean betraying my business partner, but every man for himself, I guess."

The next thing Carolyn heard was loud grunting. She turned around to see Edwin charging for them. He lunged forward and threw himself at Porter. They tumbled to the ground, Porter hitting his head on the hard floor with a loud crack. The gun flew out of his hand and he groaned holding his hand to his head.

"Carolyn, find something to bind him with," Edwin said, he was out of breath, but he had done it. "I can't see anything, so this is as much as I can help. Is he unconscious?"

"No," Carolyn said, watching Porter try to get up.

Still stunned by Edwin's show of strength, Carolyn managed to tear the hem of the wedding dress. She pushed her fear to the back of her mind and hurried to Porter's side. Quickly, she grabbed and bound Porter's wrists together, then tore another piece of cloth and bound his legs too. All the while, Porter laid there, confused. Like Edwin had wrestled the strength and his senses out of him.

"Where's the gun?" Edwin asked.

"I'll get it."

Just then, Sherman, Margaret, and Leticia sprinted into the church. Sherman picked up the gun and stared at Carolyn in both shock and relief.

"What happened?" he asked, giving his wife a hug. "Are you all right?"

"I am," Carolyn told them all with a smile. "Edwin saved me. I don't even know how he did it, or how he knew where Porter was. He just charged for him and wrestled him to the ground. It was amazing."

"I followed his voice," Edwin said. "He was talking really loudly."

"Thank you, Edwin," Carolyn said to him. "You saved us all."

Margaret wrapped her hands around Edwin's neck and sighed in relief. "Oh, thank the Lord. I was so worried, and look, I had no reason to be."

Edwin hugged Margaret tightly, burying his head in her shoulders. "I am so glad you're safe."

Sherman pulled Carolyn in for a hug. "What happened to your dress?"

"I ripped it," she said, wrapping her arms around his waist. "I can't believe I ripped it. I wanted to keep it in perfect condition. It's my wedding dress and I cannot believe I tore it."

Sherman chuckled. "I'll buy you a new one, I promise. I'm so sorry I wasn't here for you, Carolyn. I didn't know he was going to come here."

"It's all right. I see you saved Letty. That's what matters to me. Sherman, I love you, and I would do anything for you."

"I love you too," he said.

"So, is it all over?" Leticia asked, interrupting their moment. "Can I at least punch Porter in the face?"

"No." Margaret chuckled. "But yes, it's all over."

Sherman stroked Carolyn's hair and planted a kiss on her lips. "It's all over. I'll make sure of it."

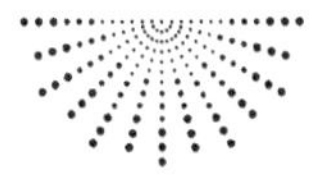

eeks later...

Leticia downed the contents of her glass and shook her head vigorously. Her cheeks hurt from all the laughter. They had been seated at the dining table in Sherman's home for over an hour having dinner. They had barely touched the food in that time because everyone had something to say. In the end, Sherman had to ask everyone to eat so the food didn't get cold.

In the past four weeks, Leticia had felt so many emotions. She was the happiest she had ever been, and the saddest at the same time. Knowing that Brandon and Porter were on their way to jail made her extremely excited. There were times before she went to bed at night that she would remember seeing them being carted away by the sheriff and she would sleep with a smile on her face. She loved to recall how defeated they looked, how ashamed they were.

Oliver had asked some of his friends in law enforcement for a few favors. He made sure that Brandon and Porter were charged not only with kidnap, assault, and extortion but also with the multiple crimes they had committed in Minnesota. They weren't getting out in a long time. Brandon and Porter knew this, and it was satisfying to see them try to beg their way out of jail time.

"So, Edwin. How's your new job at the school?" Carolyn asked him. "Are the kids treating you well?"

Edwin wiped the corners of his lips and set the napkin down. "Yes, they are. It's wonderful, I must say. A lot easier than I thought it was going to be. I love those children, and I can't imagine myself doing anything else."

"Edwin loves the fact that the children like to be around him," Margaret added. "He wouldn't stop talking about them."

Leticia smiled. Margaret and Edwin seemed happier than ever. They had not had their wedding yet, but it felt like they were already married. Carolyn and Margaret had given her a hard time when she finally told them about Oliver. They weren't angry that she didn't tell them, they were irritated they had to wait for so long to let her know they knew. But Leticia was happy that they understood. Getting over Dwight had been difficult for her, and they tried not to hassle her about love, being that they knew how much love hurt her.

"How is the owner treating you?" Carolyn asked again. "What's his name..."

"Albert," Edwin answered.

"Is he nice?"

Edwin looked down and smiled. "I think you should ask Sam that question. She is in a much better position to answer."

"Edwin," Sam rasped. "I asked you and Maggie to stop teasing me about it."

"We're not teasing you." Maggie giggled. "Edwin is right. You are in a much better position to answer that question. Don't you think?"

"No, I don't think," Sam said, blushing. "Now, stop teasing me. Albert is nice, yes. But Edwin could tell you that too. Right, Edwin?"

"I wouldn't know," Edwin said. "I don't spend as much time with him as you do."

"Stop," Sam whined. "Let's talk about your upcoming wedding instead. What's the plan? What are we doing?"

Margaret cleared her throat and held on to Edwin's hand. "Well, seeing how the last wedding I attended went, I would prefer a quick wedding. Short. Sweet. After the ceremony, we can gather like this at my house, and have dinner."

"Oh, no," Leticia said. "Why a quick wedding?"

"I'm traumatized," Margaret said.

"Well, I'm not," Leticia said. "Come on, I didn't get to dance at Carolyn's wedding, I fought a man, and I got hit in the head with a gun. I think I deserve a wedding where I can dance."

"Well, I don't want to dance," Margaret said. "I'm going to be tense all through the day, maybe paranoid too. So, no. A small wedding."

"Maggie, Porter is gone," Carolyn said. "You have nothing to worry about."

"You don't think I know that?" Margaret said. "I can't help how I feel."

"Believe me, I tried so hard to convince her that she had nothing to worry about, but she still wants a quick wedding," Edwin explained.

"Well, she's going to have to compromise because it's not just her wedding," Leticia said, taking a bite from her turkey.

"What? Last I checked, I was the one getting married, Letty. So, it's my wedding, and I say a quick ceremony."

"We'll see about that," Leticia scoffed.

"Letty," Margaret whined. "Carolyn, tell her to stop trying to change my plans. I want the wedding to end quickly so I can spend time with Edwin."

Carolyn sighed. "Well, Maggie if you think about it, you have all the time in the world to spend with Edwin. You have forever. So, how about you let us enjoy your wedding. Mine was magical, but you know how it ended. We need a cause to celebrate. The only cause in sight right now is your wedding."

"Yes, Maggie. Please?" Sam said.

"You don't need to ask her," Leticia said. "We're having fiddlers at the wedding. We are to dance all night to celebrate love, freedom, peace, and promise."

Margaret bit her lower lip. "That does sound exciting. All right, we'll have fiddlers at the party."

Everyone cheered and laughed. Leticia knew exactly why Margaret had insisted on a quick wedding. Although she was always optimistic, Margaret was easily paranoid. If she was in the same church, in the same setting where the traumatizing event took place, she wasn't going to be completely immersed in the moment. But that was the reason they were there, to remind her that she had nothing to worry about. The dance would be a good distraction.

"I think I need to say this," Edwin said. "Thank you all for changing her mind. I am so grateful because she wasn't listening to me."

Leticia giggled. "You're welcome."

And I would like to clarify something," Sherman said. He picked up his glass of wine and took Carolyn's hand. "I love you, Edwin, but your wedding isn't the only cause to celebrate."

Margaret and Leticia stared at each other and gasped. "You're pregnant, Carolyn," they chorused.

Carolyn giggled. "I am. We're expecting a baby in about six months."

"Oh," Leticia said on the brink of tears. "Oh, my goodness. I'm going to be an aunt."

The news was overwhelming. Leticia sniffed hard and batted her eyelids to keep the tears at bay. She was happy for her friends, really happy. They ate and continued to talk about the plans for the wedding and plans for the baby. When they were having dessert, Samantha tapped Leticia on the arm and turned to face her directly.

"Can I tell you something?" she asked.

Leticia turned to her. "It's about your father, isn't it?"

Samantha nodded. "Yes. I want to talk to you about my dad."

Leticia sighed. That was the only part of her life that she wasn't happy with. After the incident with Brandon and Porter, Leticia kept her distance from Oliver. She had avoided him, even in church. There were times when Oliver would come to talk to her, but she made Margaret give an excuse for her. Anything to send Oliver on his way.

Leticia was ashamed of herself. After she had untied Oliver's ropes that day at the cottage, Brandon had said that they would forever remain saloon girls, owned by

Porter Hathaway. He said they were never getting away from their past. His words had affected Leticia so much and coupled with her pent-up frustration, she let it all out. She hated that Oliver saw her that way. He already knew she held a gun to their heads in the past, and she went a step further by giving him a reason to stay away.

The truth was, she was afraid that Oliver saw too much of the dirtier aspects of her past. He had seen and experienced too much because of her.

"Letty, my dad is miserable without you," Sam said. "He is not himself and I hate seeing him like this. Can you please talk to him?"

"Sam," Leticia said softly. "I am sorry. I miss him too, a lot. But every time I think of him or see him, I remember what I put him through and it tortures me. I think he should be with someone else. Someone who isn't like me. I don't like the fact that he saw me get that angry."

"It doesn't matter to him," Sam said.

"It matters to me. Oliver is sweet. He likes me, I can tell. But I know he will never look at me the same way again. He must think I'm wild and crazy. Unladylike. That wasn't the Leticia he knew and liked."

Sam sighed and inched closer. "Letty, I need to tell you something about yourself. May I?"

"Sure."

"You leap to conclusions," Sam said. "You make decisions for other people and it's not fair. It's not fair at all. I think you're doing my father a disservice by not giving him the chance to speak to you from his heart. It's unfair. You shouldn't decide for other people. You're comfortable in your own truth, but some people need to talk about their feelings, or else it hurts them."

Leticia swallowed. "I didn't know. I'm sorry. I'll talk to him."

"Thank you." Sam smiled. "You have a connection with my father. Don't lose it."

Leticia exhaled calmly. She was still wary, and unsure how Oliver was going to treat her, but she decided to give it a try. If it was for her happiness, then wasn't it worth it?

CHAPTER NINETEEN

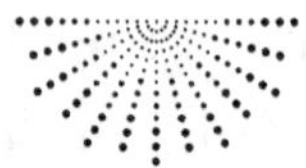

"*A*re you really going to go, or are you just saying that you will?"

"I'm going."

Leticia stood there, staring down the path. She bit her finger, too nervous to take a step forward. What if she was right and Oliver didn't want anything to do with her anymore? She couldn't blame him if he saw her in a different light. Leticia had used her own hands to paint the picture for him.

Explaining to him that she wasn't really like that was going to be hard. That was the first time she had ever hit a person. She was angry, the rage had gotten to her and she was desperate for it to be over, for it never to happen again. Would it make a difference if she told him that she was angry about him getting hurt? That she was ashamed that he got hurt because of her?

"Don't tell me you're rethinking it?" Carolyn said, crossing her arms. "Letty, for days, we have been trying to get you to visit and talk to Oliver. Now that you feel like you're ready to face him, what's stopping you?"

"Nothing is stopping her," Margaret said. "She needs to do this. It's payback for all the time she made me cover for her and lie to him that she was asleep, or busy, at the diner."

"I don't know," Leticia whined. "I don't know what to do. I think it's just best that I leave him alone. I am all right with being alone. I have made my peace with it. Not everyone achieves their dreams. Carolyn, you're having a baby. Do you know how amazing that is? I'm going to be an aunt. I can focus on that."

"Don't you dare turn this around on me," Carolyn said. "Letty, we're not going to baby you about your feelings anymore. I think it's high time you stopped letting your broken heart control you. When I had that issue with Sherman, the time I was scared that I would ruin his reputation, what did you and Margaret tell me? You said I should do what makes me happy. You both told me to go for it. It turned out that Sherman didn't even care. Look at us now."

"And when I had that issue with Edwin," Margaret chipped in. "When I was worried that he was staying away from me. You both convinced me to reach out to him. You told me he liked me, and that there was something wrong. Carolyn even went a step further and talked to him. Look at us now."

Leticia groaned loudly. "It's different."

"No, it's not. You're just being stubborn. Stop jumping to conclusions and go to Oliver. He didn't come to dinner tonight because of you. Because he didn't want to make you uncomfortable. You are quick to dish out advice but very slow to take it. It's been weeks, Letty."

"If you don't go to him right now, we'll not talk about this anymore," Margaret said. "We're going to let you be. Honestly, I am still angry that you didn't tell us when you both started courting. Instead, you kept sneaking around. Now, we're giving you advice and you're choosing to throw it away."

"I'm not throwing it away. I'm just scared," Leticia said with quivering lips. "I'm scared of rejection. That's why I let go first. I didn't do it with Dwight, and he let go of me first when I had entrusted my entire life to his hands. I don't like being rejected. I've been rejected by everything all my life. My family, Dwight, Dwight's family... It hurts. Is it that bad that I don't want to hear Oliver tell me he doesn't like me anymore?"

Carolyn and Margaret approached her. They both took her hand and smiled. "It's life, Letty," Carolyn said. "If you keep avoiding it, you will be left with questions. A lot of what-ifs. Dwight didn't reject you, you had an argument at the worst time possible. He loved you, he loved you so much. It was just an argument."

"But... we said things."

"We all say things we don't mean... that doesn't wipe out the love. If you don't go to Oliver you will be lonely and sad. I don't want that for you. Margaret and I are seeing things from a different perspective. We watched you sneak around, smile to yourself, and change your appearance. It can't all be in vain. If Oliver is in doubt, change his mind."

"You won't need to," Margaret added. "He likes you, Letty. We've seen the way he looks at you. Go talk to him."

Leticia smiled and nodded. "I will go. I think I'm in love with Oliver and I will try to win him back."

"That's the spirit," Carolyn said.

They all hugged. And the two friends stayed back and watched Leticia as she made her way to Oliver's. It wasn't helping her in any way that she was guarded all the time. Heartbreak had taught her to keep her heart shut to everything. Dwight's death had hurt her so much. It completely shattered her. So much that Leticia became defensive. Oliver was the first person to breach that wall. She couldn't let it go without a fight.

Leticia knocked on the door of the clinic and waited patiently for a response. She brushed her hair with her palm and exhaled.

"Come in," she heard Oliver say.

Leticia pushed the door open and strolled into the room. Oliver had his back to her, washing his hands in a bowl.

"Please give me a minute, I'll be right with you," he said without turning around.

"I'll wait," she answered softly.

Of course, he recognized her voice. Oliver turned around with a small cloth in his hand. At first, he stared at her blankly, his bold blue eyes nearly fixing her to where she stood. Slowly, he walked to a small sofa in the corner and sat. He tapped his side, gesturing for her to come closer. Leticia clenched her fingers into a fist and walked over to him. She sat too, and for a minute, they stayed that way, in silence.

"You really hurt me," Oliver finally said.

Leticia lowered her head and shut her eyes. "I'm sorry."

"I came to see you, countless times. I wanted to talk to you. I thought we made progress, Letty. We were special... and I really wanted you to be by my side. After the kidnapping incident, you pushed me away. You didn't even come to see me when I was sick. I got better, and I came to you instead, but you kept ignoring me. Even if I did something wrong, we could have talked about it. Why, Letty?"

Everything he said was right, and it made her feel awful for doing it. But the fact that he was talking about his feelings made her feel slightly better. It meant he still cared and that was enough for her to build on.

Leticia turned to him. "I love you, Oliver. A lot. I have ever since the day of the dance when you talked to me about my dreams and how you wanted to help me. I've never experienced something like that before and it was magical. I had never danced with someone like that before. But then I felt you pull away from me, and I raised my guard. You know how... when you're falling, let's say into a river, someone pushes you and you can tell you're going to fall. You know that thing we do when we shut our eyes and hold our breath to protect ourselves, so the fall has a lesser impact? That's exactly what I do with my heart. That day of Edwin's engagement, the way you looked at me. It made me feel like I had already lost you."

"That's my fault," Oliver admitted. "But I swear to you, I wasn't thinking about ending our courtship. I was wondering how you survived through it all. I didn't know the whole story, and I was wondering if the story I heard was sugarcoated. You looked at me the same time Margaret said yes to Edwin. My heart fluttered because I thought you wanted to marry me too. I was red all over and I looked away. I didn't mean to hurt your feelings. I was just having mixed emotions that day. But my feelings for you never faltered."

Leticia held her breath, part of her expected this was a dream and that he would say something to shatter her heart. Samantha was right. She was leaping to conclusions; even now her head told her this would fail. That night, Leticia remembered talking so much, that Oliver couldn't get a word in edgewise. She had been such a fool.

"Dwight always called me innocent," she said. "He said that was what he loved the most about me. My innocence. Sometimes, he called me pure. So, all these years, I had this notion that men wanted women that were pure. Like Carolyn, Margaret... Sam. Not girls that punch men in the face and point guns as if they mean it, threatening other people or slapping a local doctor across the face. I thought you wouldn't want to be with me because I didn't seem so..."

"Innocent?" Oliver chuckled. "Letty, I am not a child. My feelings don't just come and go. You did what you did to survive. You did what you did to save me, Letty. You hit that man because he made backhanded comments about you and your friends. I am proud of that. I'm proud that you are so strong. Why would it make a difference to me that you stood up for yourself?"

Leticia raised her eyebrows "You really don't care?" she asked.

"I really don't care." Oliver's smile waned. He rose to his feet and stood in front of her. "Wait a minute. Is that the reason you have been avoiding me? Not because of the night of Edwin's engagement?"

"I'm sorry, I am so sorry," Leticia said, covering her mouth with her hands. "As I said, I've had that idea in my head for years now. I should have known better. Please forgive me."

Oliver massaged his forehead and slowly smiled again. He inched closer to her, cupped her cheek, and placed his thumb on her lips.

"Can I kiss you?" he asked, almost in a whisper.

"Yes," Leticia whispered without hesitation.

Oliver leaned in and met her lips with his. His touch was tender and gentle, and she was filled with warmth inside as she melted into the kiss. She placed her hand on his wrist, basking in the pleasure of the euphoric moment.

Oliver pulled away and took both her hands. "I love you, Leticia Baker. I was intrigued by you from the very first day I met you. Even when you slapped me across the face and accused me of courting my own daughter, I was intrigued."

Leticia giggled. "I am so sorry about that."

"It's okay," Oliver whispered. "All is forgiven. I am grateful for you, and I want to spend the rest of my life with you if you will have me. You're incredibly beautiful, and I love listening to you, talking to you. Marry me, Letty. Please marry me."

The first thing that came to her mind was to hug Carolyn and Margaret so hard that they couldn't breathe. They deserved that much love for helping her back here so that she could experience this.

"Yes, Oliver. Without a doubt," Leticia said and hugged him.

CHAPTER TWENTY

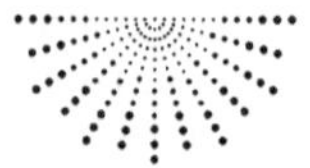

*O*ne *Year Later...*

"Are you sure you can't bring Thomas out, Carolyn?" Leticia asked.

"He's asleep."

"Well, I can carry him while he sleeps. I'm telling you, he is more comfortable in my arms."

"Do you know how hard it was to get him to fall asleep?" Carolyn chuckled. "Thomas sleeps in his cradle."

Leticia groaned and rolled her eyes. They were having dinner at Carolyn's house. It had become a monthly thing after the dinner where they had announced that Carolyn was pregnant with Thomas. Once every month, they met at either one of their homes to have dinner together. It was a great tradition that Leticia did not want to end.

Oliver kissed the back of her hand, grabbing her attention. "How about we steal Thomas tomorrow?" he asked. "Would that make you happy?"

Leticia giggled. "It would. I'll plan it all out when we get back home."

"As you wish, Mrs. Randall."

Leticia heard Sam giggling loudly and she turned to gaze at her. Sam had brought Albert as her date for the evening as she had done for the past five months. He and Sam were the same height. His midnight-black hair was always parted down the middle, and all the time Leticia had seen him, his eyes were closed, hence she couldn't tell their color. Albert was blind too, like Edwin, and they taught at the school together that Albert owned. He had been courting Sam for a year and had successfully stolen Sam from them. She was always with him, and she talked about him every chance she got.

Apparently, Edwin and Albert had made the school for the blind a thriving operation with students from nearby counties coming in every day. People from out of town brought their children to the school to learn. They had developed a new curriculum that was broader, and helped the children become better integrated and more independent.

"I need to pee," Margaret said, rising to her feet.

"You peed five minutes ago," Leticia said, shaking her head.

Margaret groaned as she rose to her feet. "Well, you would pee every five minutes if you had a child using your bladder as a pillow."

"Let me come with you," Edwin offered.

"No, I'll go," Carolyn said, standing up too. "We'll be back soon."

Leticia chuckled. She felt sorry for Margaret, but the pregnancy looked good on her. She was seven months pregnant, and she was glowing. Edwin had gotten even more protective of Margaret. He had hired someone to clean the house, to cook for her, and he massaged her feet every chance he could. They were great company when Leticia had free time on her hands.

"So, Edwin. What are you thinking of naming your child?" Samantha asked.

"Uh, Margaret and I decided on a name, and we talked to Sherman about it," Edwin said. "If it's a boy, we'll name him Sam. Samuel. If it's a girl, we'll name her Sam. Samantha."

Samantha gasped and rose to her feet. "You're naming your child after me?"

Edwin laughed. "Yes, we are. It was Maggie's idea. It's our way of remembering you since Albert seemed to have stolen you from us. And to thank you. You were the one who figured out what was wrong with me. You are a good friend, Sam. I'm happy I met you."

Leticia wiped the tear from the corner of her eye. She had a big family, one she was very proud of. They had started a new chapter of their lives together and the future seemed so exciting to think about. With no worries in the world, and a heart filled with happiness, Leticia leaned on Oliver's shoulder and held his hand. He was a safe place. Her safe place.

After dinner, Leticia and Oliver made their way home. As the wagon rolled down the street, she thought about Dwight. Her first love. She had finally achieved a level of peace and happiness she didn't think was possible. She could think of Dwight and smile as he was now a fond memory. A good one.

At the end of the day, Leticia crawled underneath the bed sheet and into Oliver's arms. He never complained about her laying on him all through the night and she was thankful for it. She liked to lay in his arms and listen to his heartbeat. During their wedding, Oliver had whispered to her after his vows, that his heart beat only for her. Since then, she was obsessed with listening to it.

"Oliver," Leticia said softly. "Can I tell you something?"

"Anything," he said, stroking her hair. "You can tell me anything."

"I was thinking of Dwight," she started. "Remembering how I used to live. I realized something. Everything is different now. I'm different. Now I understand why Margaret was so obsessed with us moving west and starting a new life, finding love. It's beautiful. I guess, what I'm trying to say is, thank you for loving me into a new life. I could not be happier."

Oliver tightened his hold on her. "Are you really happy? Is there anything I can do that will make you happier, Mrs. Randall?"

Leticia giggled. "No. Nothing at all. I am content and happy. Carolyn has a family with Sherman. That's the important part, with Sherman. Margaret and Edwin's marriage was a relationship we all saw coming from the very beginning. For me... no one saw it coming. In fact, Carolyn and Margaret were worried for me at one point. I couldn't open my heart to anyone. But I'm glad I'm past that now. I am so glad I met you, Oliver."

"We're so much alike, Letty," Oliver said. "I never thought I'd be able to open my heart to anyone ever again. After Freya left, I shut out love completely but you broke down my walls."

"You broke mine too."

Leticia lifted her head and planted a kiss on Oliver's lips.

"Does it bother you that I'm not as young as Sherman or Edwin?" Oliver asked. "I've been meaning to ask you that."

"I don't care," Leticia said, placing her head on his chest. "I fell in love with you, and that love isn't going away any time soon. We have a future together. Soon, we're going to start planning Sam's wedding to Albert, and soon they will have kids."

"What? What wedding?"

"Oh, he's going to propose soon. You know it. You've seen them together. Albert is fixated on Sam. Just the other day, he brought her expensive roses to the clinic. He brings her dresses, flowers, and food. He is head over heels in love with Sam and for good reason. Sam is amazing."

"How come I never see all these things?"

Leticia shrugged her shoulders. She had made a habit of helping out at the clinic once in a while, in whatever way she could. Leticia had confirmed the fact that she was done being a nurse, but she liked to help Oliver dress wounds so she could be closer to him. The war had completely broken them so much that becoming full-time nurses again was a repulsive thought to Leticia and her friends. They wanted to venture into other things. Carolyn was the preacher's wife, Margaret was the schoolteacher's wife, and Leticia was now the doctor's wife. All beautiful titles, but they wanted to do more. Margaret had started to quilt, and she was thinking of selling them during the summer. It was a good idea, and more importantly, it was a start in the right direction.

"Letty, do you really want to keep helping me at the clinic?" Oliver asked as if he'd read her mind. "I mean, you told me about the war and how much it affected you. I've seen you try to hold a needle. Your hands shake. I just want to be sure it doesn't traumatize you in any way. You don't have to if you don't want to. I would support what-ever it is you want to do. If you want to stop working at the restaurant, then it's fine. I'd prefer that actually, so you can spend more time at home. But I really need to know if you're all right with helping at the clinic."

"I'm all right because I'm doing it with you," she said. "I love watching you work, and knowing that I can assist you makes me happy. I just won't touch the needles or try to use them. But I can do other things. I was a nurse for years. The skills won't just go away. But I promise, if it's hard, I'll let you know. I just do it because I love you."

Oliver pecked her on the forehead. "I love you too."

Leticia snuggled into him and shut her eyes. She had no worry in the world. It was unbelievable. She had found love, and love had found her. There was a bright future for them after all. For her friends, Carolyn, and Margaret who went through so much to get to where they were. And for her, holding the hands of the man she would love for as long as she lived.

Did you miss any of this series? Grab them here or read on for an exciting preview of a reader's favorite.

A NEW LOVE FOR THE JAMESTOWN BRIDES – PREVIEW

"Russell has not said he will not marry me, Father. I can't understand why you would want to send me so far away. What have I done wrong?" Constance Dearborn wasn't crying but she was certain tears couldn't be far away.

"He has never proposed, child, and it is unlikely now that he ever will." Francis Dearborn spoke with regret. "I wish my purse was better able to cope with the times and the rising rates of expected dowries. I just can't afford one hundred pounds for one daughter, never mind three."

"And so, I am to be the one to be sent away? I am to be punished because you cannot afford to pay to have me married — well?" Constance loved her father but knew that he was much as any other father.

He was pragmatic when it came to money and the obvious burden of female offspring. But as much as that was clear, she knew in her heart that her father would not truly find it easy to watch her leave and never come back.

For surely to live in the colonies, to depart for America, could be nothing less than permanent.

"I am not sending you away, Connie. I am asking you to consider it, not only for the solvency of this household, but for yourself and your own prospects in this world."

"I had never even heard of Jamestown until you spoke the name," she said miserably, her heart hammering and the tears still threatening to fall as she stared vacantly across the room.

The sitting room in their modest home in Kensington, south of the River Thames, was small but neat. And it was the only room in their home where Constance had any recollection of her mother. If she was to leave, would she forget those last tantalizing traces of the woman who had died when Constance was just six?

But Constance knew that *that* was far from the real reason she didn't want to go. Russell Melton had filled her heart almost completely for the last two years, especially when she had realized they were within a whisper of being married.

His family had a good deal more wealth than Connie's father. Although it was true to say that Connie's father could claim gentlefolk as kin given that he was cousin to Sir Ronald Dearborn. But Connie's father whose own business had suffered from the rising cost of procurement of necessary materials, had found his own circumstances reducing year after year.

And with three daughters and no son, the expense of marrying his offspring away would be all his. Connie knew well that if the business continued to suffer as it had been doing there would be nothing left in the end, nothing for any of the three sisters to inherit. And what good was that anyway when a woman was married? Whatever her father left her would only ever become her husband's property.

Perhaps that was why Russell had not been as attentive of late. If *Constance* had worked it out, if *she* understood the world of business and how everything was likely to end in her father's case, then surely Russell had understood it too.

And if her father was right, then Russell was as concerned about a lack of his wife's inheritance in the future as he was about the lack of dowry now.

But Constance loved Russell with all her heart and it didn't occur to her for a moment to blame him for such a sentiment. After all, his family had built their wealth and a family could not continue to do that by giving an inch. And even now she could not think that he had truly decided to reject her. He had never said as much.

"I wish you would see it as I do, my dear. The idea that you would remain unmarried, scorned by everybody around you as the reverend of every church preaches the sin of spinsterhood, near breaks my heart, daughter. I should be torn in two never to see you again, but I would do that rather than have you looked down upon. At least this way you have a chance."

"Because you do not believe anybody else would marry me?"

"I do not have the resources to see all three of you suitably married, Connie."

Francis Dearborn ran his hand over his bristly chin; it made a rasping sound that was so familiar to Constance that she felt tears springing to her eyes once more.

"But you are the only one of the three who has been thwarted in love and I am certain that your feelings for Russell Melton will hold you back. Perhaps it would be a good thing for you to be far away from him where your own feelings could mend in safety. I wish I could make you understand the wonderful opportunities there are for a young woman in the Virginia Colony."

"What opportunities?" Constance asked, knowing she must at least hear him out.

"The opportunities to find a husband, and a good one at that. The settlers who left these shores some years ago have established themselves. They are the first, they will always have the richest pickings."

"But Father, I would sooner have at least some little say in who it is I am to marry."

"And you shall. That is the sincere declaration of the Virginia Company, my dear. They are offering opportunities for nicely bred women just like you to find a new life and a good husband. But I have made my inquiries well and can tell you that every lady who leaves these shores has a right to choose upon arrival. You will not be coerced into a marriage you do not want, and you may turn down as many suitors as you please. There now, is that not a good prospect?"

"Perhaps it is good if it is true," Constance said and looked down at the rug on the wooden floor of the sitting room, unable to meet her father's gaze fully. "*If* it is true."

"Will you at least give it some thought?" Francis Dearborn said as he rose from the chair with the customary groan that was more habit than anything.

"I will give it some thought, Father. But I can assure you, Russell still loves me and there is still hope." There had to be for she loved him and could think of nothing worse than to travel halfway around the world to marry a man she had never met. Marriage was about love, after all.

Jack Thornton sat on the porch of his large farmhouse in the dying light of the day and stared out across his land. He liked this time of year more than any other. He liked the way the sun clung on to the autumn day as long as it could, its orange light falling across the pale green grass of his farmland and the gently swaying corn at the further reaches.

"Staring off across your kingdom again, Jack?"

The familiar tones of Brent Stamford startled him.

Jack had been deep in thought and hadn't heard his friend approaching.

"Do you always need to creep up in such a way, Brent?" Jack asked fiercely before laughing amiably. "I reckon you will be the death of me one day."

"I wouldn't dream of it." Brent laughed too. "But let me guess what had your attention so fully."

Brent walked slowly across the porch, his worn brown boots tapping lightly on the wood as he did so.

"Probably the same thing which has every other man in town distracted."

"The women?" Jack shrugged as he knew there had been no need to say it out loud.

"What else?"

Brent sat down on the roughly hewn porch seat just feet away from his friend.

"I reckon we're all caught up in it, aren't we? Especially after last time when they sent just a few lovely ladies."

"I suppose they didn't know how it was going to go, did they? When the Marmaduke sailed up the James River I thought those poor women were going to be savaged." Jack grimaced with a hint of distaste.

"I take it you are still opposed to the idea, Jack?"

"At the time I certainly was." Jack sighed, remembering his disgust at the idea of young women being sent halfway across the world to satisfy colonists who had made the decision to leave England long ago. "But I hate to admit that it went better than I imagined."

"I remember at the time how you thought the women would be fought over, even torn limb from limb as us anxious and needy men grabbed an arm each." Brent chuckled. "And I daresay it wasn't a thought without merit."

"Had the Virginia Company not been so strident in their terms I think the whole thing might not have gone so well."

"Probably not." Brent shrugged. "But good matches were made, weren't they? These women are not urchins ripped from the streets of London, are they? They're women of reasonable breeding in a lot of cases and there was not one of them who was pressed to come here."

"Or at least none who said that she was." Jack was playing devil's advocate.

"So, now that the Virginia Company are sending more women, what do you think? For yourself, I mean?"

"It is true to say that I've given it some thought, I can't lie," Jack said, and it was true, he had given it a great deal of thought. "And I reckon that if I'm allowed to make a proposal, I might do just that."

"Now that you know these are not pressed women?"

"Yes, now that I know they are not forced into coming here." Jack laughed. "I am not at all opposed to marriages of convenience. Most marriages are marriages of convenience and they work."

"I would be tempted to say that all marriages are marriages of convenience, my good fellow."

"Perhaps they are." Jack stared out across the fields and could see the orange glow of the sun fading as he remembered one marriage that was certainly not that.

He imagined himself sitting on that same porch with a little company. Not just Brent, his dearest friend, but a wife. A wife who shared his life, his work, his bed. A partner and a companion.

"Well, I am going to try for a wife this time." Brent gazed out at the same ball of fire as it sank toward the horizon.

"You tried last time, didn't you?" Jack teased.

"And was turned down without a hearing!" Brent laughed good-naturedly; he was not a prideful man when it came to such things. "But then the ladies really did have their pick, didn't they? So many men and just twelve or thirteen women. I suppose it made sense that they did not all settle for the first man to drop to his knees."

"And did you drop to your knees, Brent?" Jack was mocking his friend but was still pleased to have Brent's company.

They had been thrown together on their voyage to the new world and they had been friends throughout the hardest times. Right from when the colony had been nothing more than unworked land on the edge of the river. The camaraderie and banter between them were vital when they were starved of other influences.

"Only figuratively speaking." Brent shrugged expansively and sighed with gusto.

"Perhaps that was your mistake? Perhaps you did not look serious enough?" Jack's chuckle was low and deep, and he felt pleasantly contented as he did at the end of every working day. That was when he took stock of all he had and everything he had achieved. It was good to be staring out across his land, and it was something he did most days.

"I shan't make the same mistake twice," Brent said humorously. "We are so short of women here that I have decided to drop down onto both knees, begging if it becomes necessary."

"Then I'll have to keep a close eye on you for that is something I could not bear to watch... or maybe I'd love to watch... I can't decide."

Jack laughed heartily now, the strain of it making his eyes water.

"You wouldn't mock a man on his knees." Brent looked outraged.

Jack laughed some more and nodded. "Okay, I promise you that I will be the keeper of your dignity, from this moment onward, my old friend. We have not suffered these barren years in the wilderness of Virginia only to crumble at the end, have we now? No, I shall be your guardian in matters of matrimony. I will not stand to see you begging on both knees."

"I only hope we do not scramble for the same woman. After so many years of friendship, I daresay the only thing that could upset everything is a boatload of pretty young women."

"Fear not, Brent. I hardly think that you and I shall grab an arm and a leg each and tug until the lady is wrenched in two."

As the two friends continued to chatter and laugh in the fading light, Jack knew that he really had overcome his misgivings over the Virginia Company's seeming trade in women. He could see it a little differently now and, more than that, he knew that his own heart had healed well enough that he was beginning to feel lonely.

Certainly, enough time had passed for him to once again look for a wife and, as he sat on the porch with his old friend, Jack decided that he would do just that.

Grab this amazing box set of 6 full length books now

INDIANA WAKE
A NEW LOVE FOR THE
JAMESTOWN BRIDES
6 BOOK BOX SET
INS OF THE PAST
EST CHOICE
ARRIOR'S HEART
TER OF LOVE
WEDDING DAY
OPEN YOUR HEART TO LOVE

The Brides of Broken Bow

If you missed any of this series, all three books are now available.
Each book covers one couple and is a complete story.

God bless,

Indiana Wake

ABOUT THE AUTHOR

Indiana Wake was born in Denver, Colorado, where she learned to love the outdoors and horses. At the age of eleven, her parents moved to the United Kingdom to follow her father's career.

It was a strange and foreign new world, and it took a while for her to settle down. Her mom raised horses and Indiana soon learned to ride. She would often escape on horseback imagining she was back in the Wild West. As well as horses, Indiana escaped into fiction and dreamed of all the friends she had left behind.

From an early age, she loved stories. They were always sweet and clean and, more often than not, included horses, cowboys and most importantly of all a happy ever after. As she got older, she would often be found making up her own stories and would tell them to anyone who would listen.

As she grew up, she continued to write, but marriage and a job stole some of her dreams. Then one day she was discussing with a friend at church, how hard it was to get sweet and clean fiction. Though very shy about her writing Indiana agreed to share one of her stories. That friend loved the story and suggested she publish it on kindle. Together they worked really hard, and the rest, as they say, is history.

Indiana has had multiple number one bestsellers and now makes her living from her writing. She believes she was truly blessed to be given this opportunity and thanks each and every one of her readers for making her dream come true.